16.91

D0890125

Angelica Lost and Found

Angelica Lost and Found

RUSSELL HOBAN

B L O O M S B U R Y
LONDON · BERLIN · NEW YORK · SYDNEY

First published in Great Britain 2010

Copyright © 2010 Russell Hoban

The moral right of the author has been asserted

No part of this book may be used or reproduced in any manner
whatsoever without written permission from the Publisher except in
the case of brief quotations embodied in critical articles or reviews

Extract from 'The Man with the Blue Guitar' by Wallace Stevens taken from
Selected Poems, reproduced by kind permission of Faber and Faber Ltd

Orlando Furioso (The Frenzy of Orlando), A Romantic Epic: Part One by Ludovico
Ariosto, translated with an introduction by Barbara Reynolds (Penguin
Classics, 1975). Introduction, translation and notes copyright © Barbara
Reynolds, 1975. Reproduced by permission of Penguin Books Ltd

Bloomsbury Publishing Plc
36 Soho Square
London W1D 3QY

www.bloomsbury.com

Bloomsbury Publishing, London, New York and Berlin

A CIP catalogue record for this book is available from the British Library

ISBN 978 1 4088 0660 9

10 9 8 7 6 5 4 3 2 1

Typeset by Hewer Text UK Ltd, Edinburgh
Printed in Great Britain by Clays Ltd, St Ives plc

To the memory of Leon Garfield

While we look not at the things which are seen, but at the things which are not seen: for the things which are seen are temporal; but the things which are not seen are eternal.

2 Corinthians 4:18

They said, 'You have a blue guitar,
You do not play things as they are.'

The man replied, 'Things as they are
Are changed upon the blue guitar.'

'The Man with the Blue Guitar',
Wallace Stevens

Contents

Preface

Volatore is a hippogriff. This animal is described by Ariosto in Canto IV, Verse 18 of *Orlando Furioso*:

> His [Atlante's] horse was not a fiction, but instead
> The offspring of a griffin and a mare.
> Its plumage, forefeet, beak, wings and head
> Like those of its paternal parent were.
> The rest was from its dam inherited.
> It's called a hippogriff. Such beasts, though rare,
> In the Rhiphaean mountains, far beyond
> The icy waters of the north, are found.

It is on this steed that Ruggiero rides to the rescue of Angelica when she is menaced by Orca, the sea monster, as she stands naked, chained to a rock on the island of Ebuda where she has been offered up as a sacrifice.

Volatore, the hippogriff, is fixated on this episode in Ariosto's epic poem. Possibly he resents Ariosto's evident delight in describing Angelica's nude plight. Passionate creature that he is, he feels that Angelica is meant to be his prize, not Ruggiero's.

Volatore has until now resided in the sixteenth-century painting by Girolamo da Carpi which hangs in the Museum of Art in El Paso, Texas. In this story he will leave the painting and travel through 2008, sometimes as idea, sometimes in human form, sometimes even as his animal self, determined to find the eternal Angelica and win her for himself. It won't be easy: Volatore is an imaginary animal but the Angelica of his choice is a flesh-and-blood woman who lives in San Francisco. How in the world – and who can say for certain exactly what this world is? – can this problem be resolved?

I

I, Volatore

Who, you may ask, is this that speaks? It is I, Volatore the hippogriff, yes! I, Volatore. I have outlived the man who imagined me into being. I have outlived centuries of little mortals who are born and die. While there are printed books and when there will be only the memory of books I shall live. What reality can compare to that? Mountains crumble, the sea is poisoned and the air but I live, Volatore, the flyer! Those others born of Ariosto's pen, Orlando, Astolfo, Ruggiero – they live also. And Angelica. Angelica! But I alone have broken through the membrane of literary reality into that of mortals. And there again I find Angelica, chained to the rock of her beauty.

Reality! What is it? Who can define it? Not those who are in it. Flying over a village I saw a little boy sitting in a toy wagon. Reaching behind him with his hand he tried to push the wagon in which he sat. When it didn't move he shook his head in disbelief.

Some have called reality a dream. The dream of reality? Who or what is dreaming it? Is it the primordial blackness that dreams reality with its colours and motion, its joys and its pains? Its sorrows? Does the blackness sleep?

2

Ravenously Seeking Angelica

Always has she been in my mind: naked Angelica chained to that so cruel and brutal rock in da Carpi's painting. Ah! her terror as she shrinks from the monster rising from the waves breaking below her. Even now I hear the screaming of the gulls, the sea-wind's moan, the roar of the great scaly Orca as he heaves himself up out of the sea. Naked Angelica, glistening with salt spray, howling into the wind, 'Holy Mary, Mother of God, let me die, I beg you, before this great beast takes me!'

How had she come to be chained to that rock from which we freed her? A homeless wanderer since the slaying of her father, the King of Cathay, she was riding on one of the shore roads not visible from the front of the picture, making for Gascony, when she had the ill luck to attract the attention of a hermit whose eyes were bigger than his shrunken member. This solitary hoper had a few demons at his disposal and he sent one to possess the horse

Angelica was riding. This sort of thing was not unusual in the world of Ariosto: travellers could take nothing for granted. Angelica's demonised steed plunged into the sea with her, swam far out with his terrified passenger, then, remotely controlled by the shrivelled satyr, brought her to a bleak strand where the hermit welcomed her with offers of shelter and refreshment.

Needless to say, once she was in his cave, also not visible from the front of the picture, he drugged her drink and attempted to perform that manly office which Ruggiero in his turn would aspire to. But, though the hermit's mind is tumescent, his manhood is quiescent. He is too embarrassed to call on demonic aid when a galley manned by an Ebudan press gang, cruising for new virgins to serve up to Orca (this is an arrangement of long-standing with the sea god Proteus which Ariosto describes in Canto VIII) carry off the frustrated ancient and his still-intact victim.

Now, while Angelica's rescue kept happening in da Carpi's painting, I went to that rocky shore deep in the distant background of da Carpi's vision and found the failed holy man, back from Ebuda, toying idly with spells and potions that gave him no satisfaction.

Holding him down with my talons I said, 'Old man, there is too much ugliness in the world and you have contributed more than your fair share. Your conduct with Angelica violated every sacred tradition of render-ing aid and comfort to travellers, and even worse, showed

4

no aesthetic appreciation. The world would be a better place without you but I'll let you live if you tell me how to move beyond the limits of time and space and take human form when needful.'

'You don't know what you ask,' said the old sorcerer.

'I know exactly what I ask and your demons will not help you if you don't answer to my satisfaction. Speak!'

'To do what you desire you must go back, back, back!'

'Back to what?'

'The beginning!'

'Of what?'

'The dream that is called reality.'

'How am I to get to that beginning?' Although I am fearless the idea of such a venture filed me with uncertainty.

'You must go through the eye of the great raven.'

'How do I find that raven and his eye?'

'He must find you.'

'How?'

'He must come to you in a dream.'

'And if he doesn't?'

'Then you can't go back to the beginning.'

'Has he come to you?'

'Nobody comes to me. I live out my days alone.'

'Now, yes, but did he ever come to you?'

The hermit ignored my question.

'I haven't even got a name,' he said piteously. 'Jerome had a name. Also a tame lion. I have nothing, even my demons have left me. Do you have a name?'

'I am Volatore.'

'Ariosto gave you that name?'

'I gave it to myself.'

'How full of yourself you are! Ariosto didn't bother to name me because my part was only to get Angelica from my bleak shore to the rock she is now chained to. He also imposed on me the humiliation of making an attempt on her virginity and coming up short.'

I was unable to offer the sympathy he craved.

'You should have been mindful of your limitations,' I observed. 'You can't break down a door with a rotten banana.'

'That comedy wasn't *my* idea! The *Maestro*, curse him! gave me lines to speak and things to do and I was obliged to speak the lines and do the things or be written out of the story.'

'*I* speak my own lines.'

'You can do that because the Maestro gave you, animal that you are, no lines to speak.'

'Don't try to be clever, old sinner. I want to know if the great raven has never come to you, how you were able to tell me how to go back, back, back to the beginning of the dream that is called reality?'

'These things are known even to those members of the sorcery community who have no importance, but we lack the virtue necessary to make use of the knowledge.'

'Very well, I'll release you now but if you have lied to me you won't enjoy my next visit.'

6

The hermit shook himself feebly when I let him go. He wandered off with no word of farewell and I departed to seek a suitable dreaming place.

I flew over sea and land, still in the world of da Carpi's painting, until I came to a sort of natural amphitheatre at the foot of a black escarpment which seemed to resound with echoes of silence under the arch of the sky.

'This will be my dreaming place,' I said. I landed in the centre of the amphitheatre and lay down to sleep. Day became night and I dreamed many things: ships and battles, knights on horseback, beautiful women, music and song. I awoke when the sun rose behind the escarpment and the second day began.

I remained where I was, fasting to clear my mind for the great raven. When night came I slept and I dreamed of sieges and towers, battles and blood, stormy seas and ships driven on to rocks where some people died by drowning, others by the sword, and the screaming of women was heard.

On the third day when night came I dreamed of blackness, only that. I dreamed of blackness every night after that, and on the eighth night the blackness swooped and became the great raven.

The great raven looked at me and blinked, showing me a clear bluish-white disc like a little round mirror in which I saw only blankness.

'Where do you want to go?' he said, and his voice rebounded in massed echoes from the black escarpment.

'To the beginning of the dream that is called reality,' I whispered.

'*Why?*' said the raven.

'I want to go beyond time and space to rescue Angelica always.'

'There are heroes for that. To me speak only truth.'

'I want her for myself.'

I was looking into the raven's left eye when I said that. Then the mirror flashed and I was in the eye looking out. Around me the vast blackness of the bird opened and lifted and the earth fell away below us, all the flimsy contrivances of humankind and the clamour of its voices blurring into dimness and distance as we rose above the grey sky and into the brilliant clarity of the blue dome in which the present curved endlessly upon itself to compass past and future.

Up we flew, high, high into the blue dome, then whistling down in a dizzying black-winged rush we shot the long, long curve past faces huge and tiny on the flickering screen of memory, faces in the shadows, in the light, lips shaping words remembered and forgotten in the moving gleams of time, the wavering of candlelight, the pattering of ghostly feet, the boom of tower clocks, the fading ink of letters tied with faded ribbons; faces wheeling with horsemen and battles and cannon, marching with armies, screaming in burning cities, drowning in shipwrecks and the thunder of the wild black ocean; palimpsested voices, distant figures and the changing colours of processions,

8

plagues, migrations, ruins, standing stones, cave drawings, jungles, deserts, dust, volcanoes, floods, ages shuffling into silence.

Down, down we arrowed blackly through the silence to a dim and smoking red that seethed and crackled and bubbled and was veined with golden rivulets of lava. Down, down through that red to a dimmer red, a deeper silence, an older stillness. We were in a cavern dimly lit by the red and flickering light of our mind, the raven's and mine.

Here, we said.

What?

Here, here, here. Our voice had become many voices, voices without number, tiny and great. The raven was no longer a raven, raven, raven, raven. Nor was I what I had been; we were without form, we were not yet alive: tiny, tiny dancing giants looming greatly in uncertain shapes and dwindling in the shadows; fast asleep and dancing in the dim red caverns of sleep.

Through age-long dimnesses of red we danced and sang incessantly the long song of our sorting: yes and no, we sang in silence, grouping and dispersing and regrouping in the circles and the spirals of the sleep-dance. Through aeons we danced while the mountains cooled under the long rains and the deeps filled up with oceans. We danced through all the colours of the years while, unseen and unknown by us, the world danced with us into the dream of reality.

The dancing continued in my mind but the raven was gone. I awoke in the centre of the amphitheatre and I knew that I could now go through time and space and assume whatever form was necessary.

3

High-Mindedness of Volatore

My aeons-long sojourn with the tiny, tiny dancing giants in the dim red caverns of sleep had made me realise how provincial my outlook had been before. How little the works of man and the hopes of man mattered and how little our dream of reality itself mattered! Still, that's all there is and we must make the best of it.

The place in which I awoke was not far from Ebuda, the Isle of Tears. Leaving my corporeality in the world of da Carpi's painting I took my leave of the amphitheatre and the black escarpment and as the naked idea of me without visible form I took to the air. No sooner had I done so than I felt a pull, as though a line connecting the centre of me to the centre of something else had grown taut. Land and sea unrolled beneath me as naked, bodiless, invisible, I was flying, flying, the cool air streaming past me until there appeared below me a noble city that I recognised at once: Rome!

When I saw the eternal city on her seven hills beneath me all gilded in the afternoon sunlight a thrill ran through me. It was springtime, the sky was blue, the world seemed beautiful. The Colosseum appeared, and from it rose the ghostly roar of the crowd as gladiators killed each other for their entertainment. This is how Nero and his Romans used their little mortal span, their little dream of reality. *SPQR, SENATUS POPULUSQUE ROMANUS*, said the standards borne by the legions. Certainly they represented the senate but what about the populace? Rome civilised the world but its roads were perhaps straighter than its politicians. From high up one looks down on what those below look up to.

I was being drawn towards the Baths of Caracalla. There seemed no danger in it as I descended to a quiet street near the ruins of the Baths. With no transition I found myself in a human mind. This was my first experience of this sort in the world of the present and 'Wow!' said who? 'You're here!' I or someone else said in white letters advancing across a blackness. It came to me that I was in the mind of someone who called himself Guglielmo Stranieri. Although I was taking in the world through his senses I found it necessary to make constant adjustments: my eyes were side by side on the front of my head so that I had to give conscious thought to the act of seeing; as an animal I had viewed things mostly from a distance; now I had to refocus; my human senses of smell and hearing lacked the sharpness I was used to, so that I was always straining to smell and hear more. The air in the room where I sat was smoky and stale, with an underscent of garlic and sweat; beyond the room I heard engines, footsteps, voices. I was/we were looking at a small free-standing illuminated window. There was no wall around it. It was on a desk beyond which were bookshelves and a wall. On this illuminated window were white letters on a black background. They formed the words you are reading now; this is how I first saw my name spelled out. There was a feeling in me as of the sap rising in a tree. 'I am part of the present world,' I said. 'I am no longer confined in a book,' and saw my words appear in this window that is called a screen.

'Why have you brought me here?' I said, and on a keyboard my fingers of Guglielmo Stranieri tapped out, 'Why have you brought me here?'

'I need you to be my friend,' said Stranieri on the screen.

I was startled by this; the idea of a friend had not so far occurred to me.

'Maybe I can make you famous,' he said.

'Ariosto has already done that.'

'But I can write a whole book about you.'

'Why are you in my dream of reality?'

'I don't know. Reality is a mystery to me and that's how I like it; an understood reality can only be an illusion.'

There was music coming from a machine. Among the voices I heard the name Alcina.

'What is that?' I asked him.

'Vivaldi,' he said. His opera *Orlando Furioso*. Do you know the poem?'

'Too well. You have read it, have you?'

'Of course. I am not ignorant.'

'So this is the connection between us.'

'I know where you live,' he said. He/I did something with a little device and da Carpi's painting appeared on the screen. 'There you are in action,' he said.

At that moment I found myself in the picture which came to life around me with the wind, the waves, the crying of the gulls, the bellowing of Orca and the weeping of Angelica. Da Carpi was standing close to her as she watched Orca with fascination and dread. 'Holy Mary, Mother of God!' she wailed. 'That monster must have a thing on him like a barge-pole! Don't let him deflower me, he'll split me in two!'

'He doesn't want to deflower, he wants to *devour* you,' said da Carpi. 'He's not after your virginity.'

'He's a male, isn't he?' said Angelica. 'And that's what all males are after. If one of them has to have me, let it be Ruggiero or the hippogriff.'

'Is sex all you think of?' said da Carpi.

'That's all the males of this world think of,' snapped Angelica. 'My beauty is the rock that I am chained to, my juiciness, my sweet flesh, my firm young breasts and bouncy buttocks, Ah!'

14

> ' "*La fiera gente inospitale e cruda*
> *alla bestia crudel nel lito espose*
> *la bellissima donna, così ignuda*
> *come Natura prima la compose.*
> *Un velo non ha pure, in che richiuda*
> *i bianchi gigli e le vermiglie rose,*
> *da non cader per luglio o per decembre,*
> *di che son sparse le polite membre.*"*

'That's what Ariosto wrote about my "lily-whiteness and my blushing roses" and all the rest of what you're staring at, that these cruel people are offering up to Orca.'

'You know Orca doesn't get you in Ariosto's story,' said da Carpi, 'so what's all the fuss about?'

Angelica was not to be pacified.

'I don't know that he doesn't get me until it doesn't happen,' she said. 'That's how real you made this picture.'

'I got beyond myself,' said da Carpi, 'I painted realer than I knew how. I never did anything this strong before and I never did anything this strong after. That's why I keep coming back to it and shaking my head in bafflement.'

---

* The harsh, inhospitable islanders
Exposed the lovely maiden on the strand.
So absolute a nakedness was hers,
She might have issued then from Nature's hand.
No veil or flimsiest of gossamers
Had she to hide her lily whiteness and
Her blushing roses, which ne'er fade nor die,
But in December bloom as in July.

'And that's why I came here to talk to you,' I said (I was speaking only as the idea of me, so I was not visible to da Carpi). 'How do you account for the power of this painting?'

'Where is that voice coming from?' he said, looking all around.

'I'm a disembodied thought. Don't let this bother you – after all, you're not quite the usual thing either, loitering in your painting centuries after your death.'

'Very well, I suppose one must make allowances. You were saying?'

'How do you account for the power of this painting?'

'I can't,' said da Carpi, shrugging his shoulders and turning up the palms of his hands.

'Try to remember who was uppermost in your mind while you worked: was it Angelica, Ruggiero, the hippogriff or Orca?'

'Volatore,' said da Carpi.

I was surprised to hear him use the name I had given myself.

'Who's Volatore?' I said.

'The hippogriff. That's what I named him.'

'Strong name.'

'Strong flier, more heroic than the hero he carried. Look at him, fearless as he swoops on the monster, carrying Ruggiero to the attack. Orca will try to bring Volatore down so he can get to Ruggiero but the hippogriff dares all. Look at him!'

As I looked, the smell of the sea and all the sounds came to me and I saw myself as the strange flying beast in the painting.

'Volatore,' said Angelica. 'I like that name and he's so big and strong and he's not afraid of anything. A woman would be safe with him.'

Keep thinking that, Angelica, I said to myself. Just give me a little time to find the right body. I tensed the muscles of my shoulders and back and they felt weak and flabby.

'Forgive me,' I said as these words appeared and the da Carpi scene dissolved.

'No offence taken,' said Stranieri. 'I know that my body isn't suitable; the bond between you and me is a different sort of thing: I shall be with you always to live your story into words. And after all, words alone are certain good.'

'Says who?'

'Yeats, top poet.'

'Well, he would, wouldn't he?'

'Never mind,' we said. 'Let's get corporeal.'

4

Stranieri Interlude

I have given some thought to the Naked-Woman-Menaced-by-Monster theme, of which Angelica and Orca are a prime example.

Always will she be there, naked on her rock, her beauty luminous in the stormy ocean dusk as she awaits the monster. Men lick their lips as the monster in each of them rises, roaring and whimpering, tasting the salt spray on her cool and trembling flesh. Angelica! Always will there be a hero to save her as the artist monsters take up their brushes.

Ingres does a chocolate-box version of the scene with a dainty hippogriff that couldn't carry two bags of groceries, let alone a hero in full armour. Doré depicts a working hippogriff that still isn't big enough. Redon gives us Angelica's tiny glowing nudity in the heart of an empurpled chaos but fudges the hippogriff. Painter after painter takes the ball hoping to score a try with this subject. Some lose it in the scrum and others fumble a pass and end up with their faces in the mud. But Girolamo da Carpi scores with Ruggiero mounted on a hippogriff that will do the job and get him there and back. Here da Carpi has abandoned the smoothness of his *Virgin and Child* – this is a different matter altogether, a he-man picture for he-men. A bit of rough, this painting, with the emphasis on Ruggiero's attack and Orca's defiance, while Angelica, relegated to the outermost corner of the picture, cowers behind her rock.

Beauty in mortal peril! Why is this theme so dear to writers and painters and film-makers? Because such beauty as remains in our world always *is* in mortal peril. And the beauty is intensified by the terror that lives in it.

The hero, of course, gets the male lead in this part of the story; he has to. But *my* hero is the hippogriff, that burly flyer as reliable as a Lancaster to bomb the shit out of Orca and get Ruggiero on to the next instalment of Ariosto's epic.

I, Guglielmo Stranieri, at my desk in the agency where I file and send out press cuttings, am not very strong and I am easily intimidated by anyone at all. And yet in some way Volatore and I are brothers. In my free time I live his life with him and word it on to the pages of this story. We need each other.

5

Dame Fortune's Decree

How to begin? I let the idea of me wander to find a useful body with a receptive mind. Wandering, wandering, no hurry, let it happen. Did the time pass slowly or quickly? Time is so various in its textures, densities, and flavours! I flowed with it, swam in it, tasted it, rose through it into the next scenes of my dream of reality.

Ecco! Here is a fine big fellow, very strong, I sense. Pictures in his mind, men locked in a struggle for a ball that is not round. On a field that is formally marked off. Wing, he's thinking. Wing is what he is. Rugby. Rugby is his game. Marco Renzetti is his name. OK, Marco! *Andiamo*!

What is this? Roma Ciampino. Being in this man's mind I think 'airport' but in my animal mind it is a monstrous thing, braying light and colour, black with noise, stinking of sweat and un-nature, ceiled and carpeted with foot-steps. Here one may eat, drink, buy every possible thing.

I, Marco Renzetti, drawn in by the glittering array of shops, buy perfume, six silk shirts, four neckties, a bottle of grappa and a little model of the Colosseum.

Now we stand behind other people. A desk. A woman takes from us what? Passport. Ticket. San Francisco is the name in our mind. San Francisco in America! Why San Francisco? No matter, this is what Dame Fortune has decreed and I must obey. Walking, walking, many people. Sitting, sitting. Through glass we see great machines. Flying soon, we think. A large voice tells us that passengers will now embark. We descend stairs and go through a little door. '*Buon giorno.*' Walking, walking, people, people. Sitting down. Fastening, with a click, a heavy belt. Music, music. A uniformed woman demonstrates what to do if the machine falls out of the sky. Waiting, waiting. Noise, vibration. We are moving, moving. My stomach lifts. We are airborne.

Very good, I have a big strong man body and I'm in a machine that flies. It's not like real flying; the wings don't move and the machine is loud and shaky as it crawls laboriously through the sky. White cloud-castles pass beneath us. Volatore, the flyer, in this unnatural flying machine. How strange to be us, living in words above the clouds. But the strangeness is all there is. There is no other place to live. From a sea of nothingness we are washed up on its empty shore, there to build our palaces on sand and dress up as whatever we think we might be.

A very pretty woman comes with drinks and little pack-ets of nuts. The scent of her flesh lingers in my nostrils, her perfume and her woman-smell. I hear the rustling of her underwear, her stockinged thighs. Short skirt but I stop my hand from sliding up. Not now. Not here. Later, if Fortune smiles on me, there will be Angelica.

In my mind something with a big oven, round slabs of dough, a long wooden paddle, an illuminated signboard, *Marco's Pizzeria*, changing to *Pizzeria Renzetti*, chang-ing to *Pizzeria Classica*. OK, Pizzeria is cool, I suppose, yes? Plain white flour in my mind, salt, dried yeast, sugar, olive oil and polenta – these are things I seem to know. Ovens, what kind of ovens are there where I am going? In my mind there is a smell of baking.

6

Pizza in the Sky, Six Miles High

This kind of flying was very slow. We ate, we drank, we saw pictures that moved: for this a screen appeared and the aeroplane was darkened. From first being seated we had been provided with a little apparatus that fitted on the head and fed voices and music into both ears. My Volatore mind was bemused by the constant presence of music everywhere. How, I wondered, did modern humankind find mental space for thought? The moving pictures before us had music and the sound of voices and large and small explosions. I removed the hearing apparatus and for a while I watched the screen on which a man ran, jumped, and drove various machines while being pursued by other men who ran, jumped, and drove other machines. Sometimes the single man stopped and fought with the other men, then he would go to a room where he had a box in which were many passports and sheaves of various kinds of banknotes. I understood that the pictures formed some kind of story imagined by whoever made up the story. But it seemed strange to me to be deprived of the pleasure of imagining one's own pictures to a story told in words. I fell asleep, awoke, consumed food and drink served on a little tray, slept and woke again. After a long time the windows tilted, I saw a great bridge over sparkling water, little sailing boats.

'First time in SF?' said the man next to me.

'What is SF?' I asked him.

It was not something I found in Marco Renzetti's mind, a mind I was not consistently in possession of; perforce I leapt from tussock to tussock of knowledge through a wide swamp of ignorance.

My neighbour laughed.

'Good question. San Francisco is just about anything you want, plus maybe some things you don't want.'

'Named for a saint, yes? A holy place?'

'Let's just say it's wholly a place, OK?'

'This is the New World?'

'It's slightly used by some not very careful owners but it's all there is. The flight attendant is coming with landing cards. Do you need one?'

'I need to land, yes.'

'Italian passport?'

'Yes.'

In my tussock-jumping I found that things I knew a moment ago were not always there in the present

24

moment; new information appeared and disappeared and left me with no firm ground under my feet.

'Raise your hand,' said my neighbour, 'and they'll give you a landing card.'

I raised my hand, got a landing card, and he helped me with it.

'Occupation,' he said. 'What do you do?'

'I was rugby, now I am pizzeria.'

'Rugby what? Player?'

'Yes.'

'But now you are pizzeria. You work in one?'

'I own one.' I had a picture in my mind of a case in the overhead compartment in which were important documents. 'Yes,' I said. 'I have to get quotes on ovens and everything must be perfect because her beauty is the rock I am chained to.'

'Whose beauty? What rocks and chains? You Italian guys must be into some really kinky S and M!'

'Sorry, I am a little deranged just now.'

'Don't apologise, there's always room for a little more derangement in SF. Myself, I like a good spanking every now and then. Does wonders for the circulation.'

'A brick oven is what I need,' I said as I felt rising in me from my feet to my brain the self-awareness of Marco Renzetti. I must have spoken that name aloud.

'Clancy Yeats,' said my companion, and shook my hand.

'The poet Yeats said that words alone are certain good,' I said.

'He was probably drunk when he said it. I wouldn't have figured you for a poetry reader.'

'It could even be that there are poets who play rugby.'

'I doubt it. Poker maybe, but nothing as rough and dirty as rugby. Where's your pizzeria?'

'In the Mission. Not open yet, just getting set up.'

'I know the best places for restaurant supplies,' said Yeats as we separated at Passport Control, 'being the owner of Clancy's Bar. Let me know if I can help with your business. Or your pleasure. Here's my card. Call me.'

I didn't think I would. In my human form I still retained some animal instincts and something about this man made me not want him for a friend. My passport and visa were in order and as Marco Renzetti I knew my way around the airport. I collected my luggage, passed through Customs, and boarded a shuttle for town.

On the bus I reviewed my position. My name was Marco Renzetti. I was thirty years old. I had been a professional rugby player, a wing with Viadana until a year ago, when I decided to leave sport and go into business while my knees were still in working order. On the advice of my cousin Giuseppe in San Francisco I bought a restaurant called Il Fornello from its owner on his retirement. On a previous trip I had looked the place over thoroughly. It was close to the thriving Delfina restaurant near Valencia in the Mission. It was Giuseppe's opinion that being a neighbour to Delfina would do us good on this busy street. The fixtures and fittings were immaculate, even to the mural of the Bay of Naples, and the price, though high, was fair. It included the apartment over the restaurant into which I could move immediately and from where I could supervise the conversion of the kitchen.

On my arrival from the airport I installed myself in the apartment and sat down to work out the details of my new venture. The kitchen conversion was the biggest expense and would be the most trouble. The picture in my mind was from my childhood in the Abruzzi: the brick oven and the wooden paddle. The next thing was to find someone who could make it a reality.

It took me three weeks to locate a man who had knowledge of such things. He was old and he wept when I told him what I wanted but he said it made him feel young again and he could do the job. When it was finished I wept remembering my childhood.

In a month I was ready to open. The blue lettering outlined in gold on the window said *MARCO'S PIZZERIA CLASSICA* and the tables and chairs waited for what the future would bring. The oven was placed so that passers-by could see me through the window as I shaped the dough and put it in to bake. Soon there were lines outside and the tables began to fill up with people waiting for my classic pizza while drinking Chianti Classico. Others came in full of nostalgia, just to shake my hand and wish me well.

I had anticipated success and had hired a pretty waitress who spoke both English and Italian and had a walk that stimulated the appetite. Giuseppina her name was, and when her lips formed her name it was almost impossible not to kiss them. I forbore during business hours but after closing time she exceeded my expectations. She was delightful but her charms were not to be compared to the immortal poignancy of the naked Angelica glistening with salt spray and chained weeping to her rock.

7

A Bit of Strange

To be a homeless idea in a borrowed body, it is like being a hermit crab in a borrowed shell. No it isn't, because that is the normal way of life for the hermit crab. This body of Marco Renzetti constricts me; I rub my borrowed shoulders, feeling for wings that are not there. Walking on my two legs I am afraid of overbalancing because I lack the other two behind me.

Ah, the sensations, the pictures in my mind! Centuries pass below me like continents, the cloud shadows race over hill and valley, mountain and sea. Above me the limitless arch of the sky, its infinite blue, and under my wings the stories of Ariosto bearing me up strongly. No, that is not now, it is a time not possible for me now. How long must this masquerade go on? When shall I find Angelica?

And when I find her must I woo her as a man? What I long for and lust for is Angelica under the real me, Angelica mounted by the hippogriff. Unlawful it may be but I am a fitter mate for her than Ruggiero or Medoro ever was and I mean to have her.

Always in my mind are the old hermit's words, 'the dream of reality'. This reality that I am living *feels* like a dream. The idea of it haunts me: to wake up from the dream of reality, this reality that is my life, would be to die, would it not? But sometimes I seem to come out of the dream, to be in another state of being, dim and red, and I do not die. Perhaps humans understand these things better than I who am only an animal. Not even a real animal but an imagined one, a fiction. Is it possible that I am mad? Can a figment of Ariosto's imagination be mad? Or am I perhaps the repository of a madness that is thus prevented from tainting the whole of the poem of *Orlando Furioso*?

The passing faces look through the window at me and I look back. The world is full of pretty women but an Angelica is rare. Her beauty, like the idea of me, transcends time and space. When I find her the years of waiting will be as if they never were; the finding of her will be as if it has followed instantly on the thought of her.

In my borrowed body I took to walking in the night. I used to go to a place that overlooked the bay. Sometimes the fog rolled in and I felt myself to be nothing and nowhere while the foghorns hooted below me like sea monsters. On the way home I passed other late walkers whose faces were like faces in a dream, each face a mystery unknown even to itself.

8

Stairway to Heaven?

One night, returning from a late walk, I chanced upon two figures struggling in a dimly lit alley. One was a man, the other a woman, and she was desperately trying to fight him off. He turned to me, reeking of vodka, and I knocked him unconscious with a single blow. She, suddenly released from his grasp, fell also. I helped her to her feet and she said, 'Wow! The answer to a maiden's prayer.'

'A maiden!' I said. 'Chained to the rock of your beauty and beset by monsters!'

'What?'

'You *are* a maiden?'

'Hold on, friend – that was a figure of speech, so let's not get hung up on personal details, OK?' She stood on tiptoe to kiss me. 'Thank you for saving me from that scumbag and you can walk me home if you like. He's not getting up; you think he'll be all right?'

'Is he someone you know?'

'No, he's a total stranger.'

'Then forget about him,' I said as she took my arm and we went on our way.

Being a man I could not help mentally undressing her and I found her beauty unimpeachable. Ariosto flashed into my mind and my shoulders itched for my absent wings as the blackness of the crow filled me, and the redness of the dim red caverns of sleep. I waited for my head to clear, then, 'Angelica!' I said.

'Who?' she replied. 'What?'

'You *are* Angelica, eternally transcending time and space?'

'Slow down, handsome. My name is Doris. What's yours?'

'Vola –' Suddenly a wave of confusion swept over me. The ball was flying through the air, I stretched out my arms and found Doris in them.

'You're a fast worker, Vola,' she said. 'I like a man who knows what he wants. Is that your first name or your last name?'

I removed my arms.

'Vola not! Name is Renzetti, Marco Renzetti.' Although I wasn't too sure of that just then.

'I like your accent, Marco. Where are you from?'

'Seven hills. Romulus and Remus suckled by a wolf. Rome.'

'Feral children! What happened to them?'

'Founded Rome.'

'Fast learners! Here we are at my place. Want to come up for a drink? I could sure use one.' She kissed me again, longer this time. 'Come on, don't be bashful.'

She unlocked the street door and as I followed her up the stairs my head cleared. Her skirt was very short, her legs beckoned sweetly and her bottom, rising before me like a full moon, cheered me on.

'Renzetti,' I said to myself, 'Marco Renzetti.'

9

Heaven's Plastic Fragrance

On entering I found myself outstared by framed prints of badly painted, miserable-looking children with huge sad eyes. The sofa was wrapped in clear plastic. From the ceiling hung a sphere made of glittering silver tesserae that spattered patterns of light on the huge-eyed children, the shelves full of tiny glass figurines, and the large television on which were plastic flowers that gave off a plastic fragrance. There were no books.

It would have been wiser on my part to go back down the stairs immediately but her going-up-the-stairs view was still imprinted on my vision.

Ah, the gulf between the real and the ideal! Ariosto's Angelica had many flaws. Her intelligence was a sort of low cunning with which she evaded pursuers. She used her beauty unashamedly to manipulate men. She made promises she never kept but pursuing her was time well spent. To speak modern, she was a class act.

The portents were not favourable, my chance of success extremely doubtful. In my quest for the timeless and eternal Angelica I was well aware that Ariosto had married her off to Medoro who became King of Cathay. I persisted nonetheless.

As Volatore/Marco Renzetti I found life confusing. As a hippogriff I had been chaste, being only a means of transport; carnal pleasures were reserved for my heroic passengers. As a man I had been initiated into human practices by the frolicsome Giuseppina. She was generous in her praise of my performance; so I ought to have been easy in my mind with Doris Donner.

She was a hairstylist at Salon Angélique (the random irony of names!) and she took pride in having styled the hair of Lola Trotter, the film star.

'The studio stylist got the credit,' she said, 'but all he did was add highlights to what I'd already done.'

More beautiful than the 'supermodels' who appeared in the news, Doris had only contempt for them.

'These girls have arms and legs like sticks,' she said, 'and the fashion industry is run by faggots.'

The women whose looks she looked after, except for a few celebrities, did not fare much better in her opinion.

'Some of them have had so many facelifts their ears meet at the back,' she said, 'and they want me to do some miracle with their hair so their husbands will look at them again. Meanwhile the husbands are shtupping their twenty-five-year-old secretaries. You can't make a silk purse out of a sow's ear but you can make millions by telling the sows you can.'

Doris's cynicism did not extend to sex. I was overwhelmed by the frequency of her demands; she was not so much chained to the rock of her beauty as rolling it after me so that I was in constant danger of being crushed by it.

Doris was what she was, coarse despite her physical refinement, definitely not my eternal time-and-space-transcending Angelica. Why, then, did I stay with her as long as I did?

Nobody's perfect, as they say, and I admit to my shame that Doris for a time distracted me from the search to which I had dedicated myself. As Marco Renzetti I was only human and as Volatore I was equally susceptible to beauty. Doris was a head-turner, like the girl in the song who makes everyone say 'Aah!' when she passes. A trophy, and I was proud to be seen with her on my arm when we went out. Which Doris liked much more than staying in. She introduced me to what she called 'the club scene' and we went to the DNA Lounge to shake ourselves about in what they called dancing. As Marco I had done this before and Doris was pleased with how well I fitted into this pathetic hyperactivity.

I arranged our next outing: we went to the San Francisco Opera where I had the pleasure of hearing *Madame Butterfly* by my countryman Giacomo Puccini, sung in my native tongue by an excellent cast. Doris and I both had tears rolling down our faces when Cio-Cio San sang '*Un bel di vedremo . . .*'

'That son of a bitch Pinkerton,' said Doris. 'He knocks her up and then it's bye bye, Butterfly. Men are basically rotten.'

'Unfortunately that's the way of the world,' I said. 'Women aren't much better but people are all there is to work with.'

'Tell me about it,' said Doris. 'I do their hair.'

When Cio-Cio San killed herself with her father's sword in Act III Doris wept again, but more in anger than in sorrow.

'I'd have used that sword on Pinkerton,' she said.

'He wasn't there.'

'I'd have tracked him down and cut his balls off,' she said with a shake of her head.

'How did you like the music?'

'There were a couple of nice tunes but it was a long time between them and you don't know what they're saying unless you read the libretto. Opera isn't really my kind of thing.'

Doris liked sports, so we went to Candlestick to see the heavily padded 49ers, protected by everything but airbags, play American football. But whatever we did we did as Marco and Not-Angelica. She said she loved me but her love was meaningless to me. To have before me a simulacrum of Angelica without her essence was a mockery and I enjoyed her body as one enjoys a whore.

By this time I had acquired a second baker, Luciano Strozzi, the man who had built my oven. My cousinly obligations with Giuseppe were few and far between, so I began to learn my adopted city, travelling by foot or public transport.

San Francisco, heroic city that sits on its tragic flaw, the San Andreas Fault! With my animal senses I could feel the play of the tectonic plates under my feet and the rasp of their constant shifting, smell the vapours beneath. I could hear the ghosts of the Barbary Coast cursing and shouting and singing lewd songs up through the restless stones.

Doris told me that there was a 62 per cent probability of a major earthquake between 2003 and 2032.

'This really isn't a safe place to be,' I said.

'No place is safe,' she said. 'You could get hit by a bus crossing the street. We could both be dead before the next quake. Anyhow, these people who make the predictions are wrong as often as they're right.'

So we dropped the subject.

San Francisco is a city that Ariosto might have imagined, of impeachable reality, existing by enchantment and never to be taken for granted. Everything about San Francisco is metaphor, from the magic span of the Golden Gate Bridge to the up-and-downness of its streets where the cable cars, laden with passengers inside and out, clang their bells as the driver grasps the cable that hauls them up to the heights and down to the depths of their desires.

This metaphoric San Francisco has its own acoustic in the sun and the rain and the fog, in the lights of its nights and the darks. And it talks to itself constantly.

The voices! Sometimes I immersed myself in the exotic inflections of Chinatown, understanding nothing but taking in the music. At the Taquería Cancún in Mission Street I listened to the easy cadences of Spanish while tasting the language in a burrito.

By now I was spending more nights in solitary walks than I was with Doris. Clearly our time together was coming to an end but I thought that in all fairness I should consider if perhaps there was more to her than I gave her credit for. I decided to ask her the big question one night as we lay in bed after our usual embrace.

'Doris,' I said, 'would you love me if I were a hippogriff?'

'What's a hippogriff?' she said.

From the drawer of the bedside table I took a small print of the da Carpi painting and showed it to her.

'That's an animal,' she said.

'But could you love it?'

'You mean, like a pet?'

'No, I mean the way you love me in my present form.'

'You mean, have sex with it?'

'Yes.'

'No way! You're talking perversion.' She made sounds of disgust, kissed me goodnight, rolled over and went to sleep.

There was nothing more to be said. I slipped out of bed and in less than an hour I was gone.

10

On Wings of Song

What now? I had no idea. I was walking the streets aimlessly when I heard singing. In my mind there opened the skies and the seas of *Orlando Furioso* in which Olimpia, left on the beach, laments her abandonment as Bireno sails away from her. '*Voglio, voglio morire . . .*' she sings. '*Oh Bireno, Bireno!*' Here, now, on a street in San Francisco! Her voice rose in me and lifted me above the centuries that passed beneath me. Once more I was the animal of me, Volatore the hippogriff! Like a snake shedding its old skin the idea of me slid up out of Marco Renzetti.

I was looking through an open window at a beautiful young woman in her underwear. She was doing exercises, her long red hair swinging with her movements. Ah, the beauty of her! How it pierced my heart! At once imperious and vulnerable, demanding to be protected, to be saved. Chained, yes, chained to the rock of her beauty.

Be careful, I told myself. Remember Doris.

Heedless, I called out, 'Angelica!'

She looked up and gave a little shriek but made no move to cover herself.

'Holy smoke!' she said. 'Am I hallucinating you?'

'No,' I said, 'I'm real.'

'That's one hell of a real smell you've got!'

'That's how a hippogriff smells.'

'A hippogriff. That's what you are?'

'Yes. Have you read *Orlando Furioso*?'

'Give me a moment to compose myself. Your head, your eyes and your beak are very unsettling to look at, and with the smell you take some getting used to.'

I gave her a moment. She composed herself and seemed to be getting used to me.

'Does my smell offend you?' I asked her.

She stood there wordlessly, taking deep breaths, then she said, 'No, but it's having a strange effect on me.' She poured herself a large whisky, arranged herself on a sofa so that her near-nakedness and her graceful limbs showed to best advantage, drank about half of the whisky, sighed, and said with as much aplomb as if she entertained hippogriffs every day, 'How do you know my name?'

'Is your name really Angelica?'

'Not an uncommon name, actually.'

'Ah, but this is a fated meeting!'

'I've heard that before.'

'But I speak from the heart!'

'That too. You mentioned *Orlando Furioso*.'

'Have you read it?'

'Yes, but more than that, I have dreams where I'm chained to that rock on the isle of Ebuda with Orca rearing up out of the water and coming at me.'

'Then you *are* Angelica!'

'Angelica Greenberg, not the one in *Orlando Furioso*.'

'Angelica is more than the words of Ariosto, she goes beyond time and space and the boundaries of language; her story is in you, and in your dream you know that you will be saved by me and Ruggiero.'

'No, I don't. Nobody saves me.'

'What happens?'

'I wake up. Otherwise I wouldn't be here, would I?'

'Yes! You need have no fear of that dream, Angelica! Always I'll be there to save you! With Ruggiero in the saddle, of course.'

'Yes, but that's in a story, an epic poem, and this is real life, I think. How'd you break out of the story and get to my window?'

'It would take a long time to tell you.'

'Did you fly here? I'm three storeys up.'

'The singing lifted me, the voice of Olimpia lamenting her abandonment by Bireno.'

'Emma Kirkby. She's remarkable. I listen to that recording a lot.'

'Olimpia is so sad. Are you sad?'

'Isn't that the human condition?'

'Olimpia is sad because she's been abandoned by Bireno. Has someone abandoned you?'

'Yes, as a matter of fact someone has.'

'Who could sail away from *you*?'

'Even with the smell you're a real smoothie, aren't you?'

'How did it happen, this abandonment?'

'I don't believe this: I'm hallucinating a hipposhrink.'

'You mock me. You are the eternal Angelica and you tell me that your life is sad. Are there no intervals of joy?'

'Is that what you are, an interval of joy?'

'May I speak modern?'

'Please do.'

'Are you coming on to me?'

'Why do you ask?'

'You were almost naked when I arrived and you have not covered yourself since; rather you offer yourself as a feast for my eyes.'

'Because I want you to keep looking at me. As long as I feel your eyes on me I think we're both real. Maybe.'

'You doubt your reality?'

'Constantly. Don't you, being imaginary as you are?'

'I am as real as Ariosto imagined and that is enough for me. I try not to question it.'

'How strange this is!'

'Strangeness is all there is. May I come in? I feel rather exposed out here. My name is Volatore.'

'How do you do. I'm Angelica Greenberg. But I've already told you that.'

'I ask again, may I come in?'

'First tell me where you're coming from.'

'Geographically, or are you speaking modern?'

'Either, both, whatever.'

'I'm coming from the isle of Ebuda.'

'But you didn't fly here out of *Orlando Furioso*, did you? That's literature; this is San Francisco.'

'I walked from the Mission.'

'How come?'

'That's a long canto and I'm still outside here for all the world to see.'

'Sorry, I'm forgetting my manners. Come in and have a cup of tea.'

'If I can get through the window.'

'Think small.'

I folded back my wings, thought small, and squeezed through the window.

'I'm afraid my talons will tear up your rug,' I said.

'Not to worry, hippogriffs are scarcer than kelims.' She stared at me for a few moments, then went to the kitchen and put the kettle on.

I looked around me at her flat. Many books, colourful cushions on the sofa. A framed print on the wall that was strangely evocative but confusing, an empurpled chaos with a little naked woman glowing at the heart of it.

I called to her, 'What is this picture?'

'*Ruggiero Rescuing Angelica*, by Odilon Redon,' she said as the kettle whistled.

'As I look more closely I see myself in it,' I said, 'but he could have represented me more powerfully.'

'With a symbolist,' she said, 'you have to take the thought for the deed.'

'Nevertheless, this picture is yet another sign that this *is* a fated meeting, or at least a fateful one.'

'Remains to be seen,' she said as she came into the room with the tray and tea things, but I could already feel what Doris called chemistry between us. Angelica gave me the tea in a bowl so that I could dip my beak. 'Now that I see you up close it's a lot more startling than when you were at the window,' she said. 'Your eyes, your beak, your smell . . .' She looked away, and began to hum a tune.

'What are the words to that tune?' I said.

Still looking away from me and blushing, she said very quietly, 'They're just something about a wrong time, a wrong place, a wrong face and a strange attraction. Nothing about a wrong smell.' Her fragrance was maddening. I felt her warm breath on me.

'*Is* there a strange attraction?' I said.

Almost in a whisper, her face still averted, she said. 'I feel kind of crazy, so if you're going to make a move, do it now before the feeling goes away.'

'I'm not sure what to do,' I said. 'I don't want to frighten you.'

'Please don't look at me directly, you make me feel weird.'

'In what way?'

'More like an animal than usual.'

'And?'

'I'd rather not say.'

'Say!'

'I'd like you to kiss me but you can't because of your beak.'

'I think I can change to human form if you want me to.'

'No. I want you as you are.'

'You *want* me, really? Is that what you're saying? I can scarcely believe my ears – I never dared hope, so soon, that this could happen.'

'First we have to see if it's a practical possibility.' She was inspecting my genitals. 'Jesus! you're hung like a horse.'

'Like a hippogriff, actually.'

'Could you think a little smaller?'

I thought a little smaller while she watched the process. 'Stop,' she said. 'That should be about right.'

She removed her underwear and got down on all fours like a submissive mare. Her naked back and breasts, seen from behind, filled my eyes, my mind and my very soul with their femaleness. And at the same time I was thinking, Ariosto imagined me. Did he imagine this?

'Here I am,' she said softly. 'Take me.'

46

So seductive she was! So delicious, so full of desire as I mounted her! She gasped and cried out when I entered her but soon she was moving with me and voicing her pleasure. And I! This was the happiest moment of my life. To how many of us is it given to be wanted for what we truly are! And to be loved for our true selves! And she *did* love me, I could feel the very soul of her in my embrace. Her orgasm went on and on until she was exhausted. When I withdrew she remained on her hands and knees, swaying a little.

'Are you all right?' I said.

She turned her face to me. She was smiling with tears streaming down her cheeks.

'When you came, when I felt your seed spurt into me, I saw the shadows of great wings on a sunlit meadow; I seemed to be remembering it from a long way back.'

'I come from a long time back, my love.'

'Yes, I am your love and you are mine. You're an imaginary beast from an epic poem by Ariosto. You were an imaginary beast when you mounted me and you're the same talking to me now. Volatore, how is it that a real woman can mate with a poetic invention?'

'Everything is real, Angelica. Reality is a house of many rooms, and sometimes we can enter more than one. Ariosto's words put real wind under my wings, made me fly. It was not only words on paper – I remember the air rushing past me, remember looking down on plains and forests, mountains and oceans. I lived, I flew over the sea in a painting by Girolamo da Carpi in a time long past. You and I are both in the world of that picture which lives even now and waits for us here in this country, in El Paso. And in the same Now here I am in your mind or in a dream, I don't know. But you felt my weight on you, felt me inside you in our dream of reality.'

'If we could couple as we did, mind and matter, waking and dreaming, might we produce an offspring?'

'I don't know, Angelica. I don't know the boundaries of this reality.'

'Maybe our child . . .' she started to say. She was still on her hands and knees. Then, 'The figures in the carpet are dancing all around me.'

'Our child, Angelica?'

'Maybe our child will be a story,' she murmured. 'A story will be our only child.' And she began to weep.

I tried to comfort her.

'We have each other,' I said. Lamely.

'I want you to hold me and kiss me and cuddle me,' she said. 'Can you put on a human shape for me?'

'Tell me something first, Angelica . . .'

'What?'

'Tell me again that you are my love.'

'Yes, Volatore, I am your love.'

'And you truly love me, heart and soul?' As the words left my beak I felt the swoop of a great blackness.

'It's all so strange!' she cried. 'Please!' she said again, 'I need you to kiss me and cuddle me before I can be sure.'

'Wait here and I'll leave my hippogriff shape and find a man body and come back to you.'

'I'll come with you; after all, I should have the choosing of the man I'm going to be intimate with. When you beome a man, how shall I know it's you?'

'I'll say, "Here is Volatore."' I became the idea of me with no visible form and we set out.

Angelica was of course chained to the rock of her beauty and monsters of all shapes and sizes came thick and fast, some with honeyed words and some with lewd proposals. She rejected one after another; when any became offensive I showed them my full hippogriff self and they left pretty quickly. We wandered up and down and by winding ways and eventually came to the place that overlooks the bridge and the bay.

A man was standing there with his back to us.

'You've come at last,' he said to Angelica.

Was there something? What?

'You were expecting me?' she said, looking him up and down critically.

'Yes, I was. Sometimes I get a little crazy. I told myself that if I come and stand here night after night a beautiful stranger will appear.' His breath. Vodka.

'Maybe,' said Angelica, 'I won't always be a stranger.'

'No!' I said. 'Wait!'

11

The Buttocks of Giuseppina

'Whoosh!' says Marco. He suddenly feels as if something has gone out of him, leaving him in some way a new man, light and easy, refreshed and invigorated. 'Wow!' he adds.

'*Che*?' says Strozzi as he slides a pizza in to bake.

'Where?' says Marco, standing in the pizzeria that bears his name.

'Where what?' says Strozzi.

'Who?' says Marco as Giuseppina, pizza-laden, sways past him. Coming back to himself in a flash, he affectionately squeezes her left buttock.

'What's this?' she says. 'You've just now rediscovered my *natica sinistra*? I have one on the other side also. They're a matched pair.'

Marco bilaterally embraces her bottom and draws her to him.

'*Piano, piano*,' says Giuseppina, 'the pizza's getting cold. See me after closing time.'

'Sweet Pina!' cries Marco as the joy of life and the vital sap of the vernal season rise in him and he follows her into the dining room. 'I feel as if I've been away for a long time but now I'm back, and only now do I realise all that you are to me! You are my basil and my oregano! You are my mozzarella!'

The diners look up from their pizza classica and give the couple their full attention.

'I've seen nothing of you and heard nothing from you for weeks,' says Giuseppina with the colour mounting to her cheeks, 'and do you mock me now?'

'I do not mock, Giuseppina! I love you!'

'You're embarrassing me! Be serious, *padrone*!'

'But I *am* serious!'

Her eyes narrow as she serves the pizzas.

'How serious?'

Marco goes down on one knee and there is a collective intake of breath from the onlookers.

'Go for it!' urge the assembled upholders of traditional family values.

Marco goes for it.

'Marry me!' he demands in ringing tones that make passers-by in the street turn their heads and smile.

'You hear this?' says Giuseppina to the breathless pizza-goers. 'What answer shall I give the *padrone*?'

'Yes!' they shout as one.

Giuseppina raises Marco to his feet, kisses him soundly,

places his hands firmly where they have been longing to go, and breathes softly into his ear, 'What's mine is yours.'

Cheers and applause. It's like something in a movie.

12

Figs with Cream!

Vassily, his name is. A big man and no gentleman, reeking of Stolichnaya the same as on the night he attacked Doris. I knocked him out then, so why don't I become my hippogriff self now and let him feel the weight of my talons?

Right! Here I go. Nothing happens, I'm still an invisible idea. Only a little while ago I was seeing off unwelcome suitors with my full self but suddenly I don't know how to do it. Was there a magic word? Meanwhile Angelica was breathing in his stinking breath and looking at him with desire in her eyes.

All I could do was climb into his mind, and it was so swollen with his single intention that it was a tight squeeze.

'Here I am,' I gasped to Angelica. 'Here is Volatore.'

'What's your name, handsome?' she said playfully, as if sharing a joke with me.

'Volatore, Volatore!' I tried to say, but the name that came out was 'Vassily'.

'Sure you are, but you're my Volatore, yes?'

'Who's Volatore?' said Vassily.

'*You* are, aren't you?' said Angelica.

'I'll show you who I am pretty quick as soon as we get out of the weather,' said Vassily.

We, the three of us, went to where his red Mercedes was parked. It had doors that opened like wings.

'Classy set of wheels,' said Angelica. 'This is a 300 SRL.'

'You can depend on me for a good ride, *golubchik*,' he said (I was unable to make myself heard).

'I believe you, Volatore.'

'Vassily, baby.'

'OK, Vassily Baby.'

We got in and Vassily put his hand on her leg.

She put her hand over his.

'Don't be shy, Vassily Baby,' she said, and moved his hand further up her thigh (I could do nothing). 'Have we got time for a kiss and a cuddle right here?' she said.

'For this there is always time,' said Vassily, and she came into his arms (I, Volatore, felt that hot embrace.) Tasting the sweet mouth of my erstwhile love, Vassily recalled a favourite dessert of his childhood: figs with cream. That was how she tasted, his delicious Angelica.

'"Wild thing!"' she said. '"You make my heart sing!"' (This from the woman who had declared herself my love only moments ago. Was eternal Angelica forever unreliable?)

'I'll get to your other parts right away.' (The *coarseness* of the man!) 'Excuse me for just a moment,' he said as he stopped the car. 'Call of nature.'

Vassily stepped behind a bush, dropped his trousers, there was a little straining and I, Volatore, was expelled, hitting the ground as a full-size hippogriff. Then Vassily got back in the car and drove off with Angelica.

So easily had Vassily Baby disposed of Volatore the hippogriff!

I tried to revert to the mode in which I was idea without visible form but I was unable to do it. How had the Russian been able to expel me like that? Had the idea of me become so weak that an ordinary human was stronger than Volatore the hippogriff?

Fortunately the hour was late and there was no one about. If only I could fly out of this situation! But I had no winged words to lift me. Trying hard to think small, I crept away in the dark, cursing and whimpering, seeking a place to hide.

13

Extruded, Excluded and Bewildered

Many scents came to me: animals; grass; trees; flowers; fresh water; wooden buildings; bushes. I smelled my way to a great park and there I hid myself in the bushes and tried to think what to do next. I was distracted by a roaring, then I realised that I was doing it: my loss was too great for words. Only roaring and the outpourings of madness could express it. To find Angelica after long centuries only to lose her after a brief moment of happiness! Only those who have possessed and immediately lost the fulfilment of their hopes and desires can know my despair.

Then my lamentation turned to rage. How could Angelica, after what had passed between us, drop me and go off with Vassily Baby! Faithless slut! How could I ever trust a woman again! No, I mustn't think that, there must be some explanation for her behaviour that will eventually reveal itself to me. Perhaps my power had faded and needed recharging – that would explain much. But not Angelica's acceptance of Vassily Baby as her lover.

What to do now? No idea; I couldn't be invisible and I couldn't fly. And I was hungry. Following my nose I found large, shaggy, horned cattle which I could have killed, but they were too big to be eaten in a single meal and I didn't want to keep a carcass that was starting to smell. I contented myself, therefore, with such smaller cattle as I could find: frogs; toads; lizards; mice; ducklings. I required a great deal of this sort of provender, so I hunted every night in areas of the park not frequented by visitors or homeless men.

This was certainly a low period in my life and I could see no end to it. I tortured myself calling to mind Angelica, naked, waiting on all fours for me to cover her as the griffin had covered my mother.

'Yes, Volatore,' she had said, 'I am your love.'

I4

Up, Up and Away, But . . .

Sometimes the fog came rolling in off the bay, heightening scents and muffling sound. It rested on my face like the touch of Time's hand and I felt lost and alone. My existence is so tenuous that it could be snuffed out like a candle by any unfriendly wind. If the vital connection between me and Angelica were broken . . . but I dared not think of that. Nevertheless I *did* think of it and everything else: the raven in whose mind I live and the tiny, tiny dancing giants in the dim red caverns of sleep. I had broken through the membrane that divided the reality of the imagination from that of the tangible world and only now did I question my right to do so. This world, whatever its reality, is held together only by consensus, by everyone's agreeing to abide by rules arrived at by trial and error over the centuries. I had broken those rules, I was an ontological outlaw and I was suffering a just punishment.

But one foggy night I smelled – was it truly, could it be? Yes, it was! Angelica! Her voice came softly through the mist. My soul was irradiated with hope.

'Volatore!' she called. 'Volatore!'

The park was deserted. I made my way to the overlook. The bridge was invisible; the foghorns hooted like lost sea beasts. There she was, my? Angelica.

'No Vassily baby tonight?' I said.

'Only you and me,' she answered.

'For how long? An hour? Two?'

'For as long as we're allowed.'

'By whom? By what?'

'By the story that we are part of.'

'Really! And was your time with Vassily a chapter in that story? You abandoned me and went off with him. How could you do that?'

'At first I thought he *was* you. I kept calling your name but you didn't answer. He was all over me, hot and heavy, and I lost my head. I was confused and all stirred up and I wanted satisfaction, I'm only flesh and blood after all. Can you understand that?'

'I can understand one time, but you've been with him night after night.'

'No, I haven't. He's not a very nice man and I got away from him after that one time. I've had some gallery business to catch up with and since then I've been looking for you. Which hasn't been that easy. Now that I've found you can you forgive me?'

'If it was only the one time.'

'It was. Listen to this.' She had a book in her hand, and by the light of a little torch she began to read:

> '"*Non è finto il destrier, ma naturale,*
> *ch'una giumenta genero d'un grifo*:
> *simile al padre avea la piuma e l'ale . . .*"'

A thrill ran through me like electricity, I felt the blood coursing through my body as my wings stiffened.

'That's the hippogriff in *Orlando Furioso*!' I said. 'That's me! You've brought me Ariosto!'

'So are we going to fly out of here or what?'

It took me a moment to grasp the reality of this new situation.

'Yes,' I said, 'we're going to fly out of here.'

'Where to?'

I was taken aback by her direct question. I had given no thought to a destination. Back into the world of da Carpi's painting? No, that was the reality I'd broken out of to get to San Francisco. Angelica had spoken of what we were allowed by 'the story we are part of'.

'Here, then,' I said to her, 'is an anomaly: we purpose using Ariosto's words to power our flight out of Ariosto's story.'

'But we're already out of his story, aren't we? San Francisco isn't in *Orlando Furioso*. I'm having a hard time getting my head around this! What do you think we should do?'

60

I closed my eyes and the golden sunlight of Rome, its seven hills and the ruins of the Colosseum flashed into my mind.

'Rome!' I said. 'We'll fly to Rome on the Maestro's words and continue our own story there.'

'Do you think we'll get away with it?'

'"*Dum spiro, spero,*" baby, if I may speak classical and modern at the same time.'

'Gimme an asterisk.'

'"While I breathe, I hope."'

'You're one ballsy guy, Vol.'

'Hung like a hippogriff, *piccina*.'

'It's all very well to kid around but this thing we're doing could be the end of us if it goes wrong.'

'Let's just do it, OK?'

'Can you navigate in this fog? There's no visibility at all.'

'We'll climb above it.'

'Yes, but you must remember not to fly over the island where Angelica is chained to the rock.'

'I'll remember. It gets cold high up and it's a wet night. Will you be warm enough?'

'I'm wearing a heavy woollen sweater and foul-weather yachting gear, OK?'

'You'll have to hold on tight – there's no saddle or bridle for you.'

'Not to worry – I've got rope to tie myself on with.'

'Do that and tell me when you're ready for take-off.'

'Ready now.'
'Start reading again.'

> ' "*Non è finto il destrier, ma naturale,*
> *ch'una giumenta genero d'un grifo:*
> *simile al padre avea la piuma e l'ale,*
> *li piedi anteriori, il capo è il grifo;*
> *in tutte l'altre membra parea quale*
> *era la madre, e chiamarsi ippogrifo;*
> *che nei monti Rifei vengon, ma rari,*
> *molto di là dagli aghiacciati mari . . .*" '

I felt the power in my wings and there came a rush of
air beneath me as we rose into the fog.

'Yes, oh yes!' said Angelica. 'Welcome to Volatore
Air!'

Once above the fog I was able to see the North Star
and the Wain and I set my course for Italy with a cold
wind against us.

'This is like a dream,' Angelica shouted above the wind
and the whoosh of my wingbeats. 'I think we are in our
own time which is outside of time.'

'We are together, that is enough.' I had some doubts
about the outcome of our flight but I kept them to myself.

'But there's something you have to understand. Listen,
Vol – is it OK if I call you Vol?'

'It's cool. I can speak modern but I must not lose
altitude.'

'About our togetherness – I'm not a reincarnation of Ariosto's Angelica, I'm Angelica Greenberg and I run a San Francisco art gallery in the year 2008. And I have to say I'm a lot nicer than Ariosto's Angelica. He himself says, "She holds the world in such contempt and scorn,/ No man deserving her was ever born." She uses men when she needs help, she makes them think she's hot to trot, then as soon as she's safe she's off without so much as a goodbye kiss. To put it crudely, she's a cock-teaser.'

'The ordinary rules do not apply to her. She is beyond such limitations.'

'That may be but she's nothing like me.'

'No matter; the idea of Angelica may manifest itself in various ways but it persists and you are it.'

'All right. Let's talk about you for a moment. Apparently you're making your own decisions now but in that part of Canto IV that I read you Atlante was your master.'

'That necromancer! Although by artifice he made me do as I was bid, my heart's desire from him I kept well hid.'

'Vol, you're speaking like the English version of *Orlando Furioso*.'

'Sometimes emotion makes me slip into rhyme.'

'Have you flown this route before?'

'Probably. I don't remember.'

'Atlante used to do the navigating, right?'

'Angelica, what are you getting at?'

'The anomaly you spoke of earlier – we're trying to get away to our own story by flying on the power of Ariosto's words, right?'

'Right. We talked this over and decided to chance it.'

'I think our plan's not working. Call it woman's intuition. Keep on flapping your wings and we'll find ourselves over that island where Angelica's chained to her rock and Ruggiero's riding to her rescue on your back.'

'I won't allow that. From this time forward I am my own hippogriff.'

'That's as may be, but there's another thing that's bothering me. Maybe this is the wrong time to bring it up.'

'What?'

'Vol, sweetheart, tell me, what sort of future can we have together, in or out of this story: an imaginary beast and an actual woman? You and I might couple from time to time but we don't constitute a proper couple. I'm only human and I ought to have a human lover.'

She was voicing the doubts that had long been lurking at the back of my mind but now I was too preoccupied to answer. Oceans and continents sped beneath me faster and faster. Something was pushing me in a new direction.

'Well,' shouted Angelica, 'I'm waiting to hear your thoughts.'

'We can't go into that now. I'm being forced off my course.'

'I was afraid this was going to happen. What are you going to do?'

'Whatever I can. Don't distract me.'

'We're over water – are you going to ditch?'

'Quiet! I have no control whatever.'

The water was behind us and the ground was coming up fast.

'There's that lousy island with Angelica chained to her rock and that monster with a hard-on,' shouted Angelica. 'Ugh, I can smell him from here. Oh God, are we going to crash?'

'Worse, I fear. Try to prepare yourself.'

Even as I spoke she found herself chained to the rock, clothing and foul-weather gear gone, naked as the day she was born. Orca's roars took on a throaty note.

'What's happening to me?' she wailed. 'Am I the original Angelica now?'

I was too busy to answer, finding myself saddled and bridled with Ruggiero in charge of me. He put me into a dive but he was overly cautious and pulled me up too soon. His lance did little more than scratch Orca's back, and the monster laughed at us as we flew up out of harm's way.

'You're some hero!' I said to Ruggiero, lapsing into modern. 'Why don't you hit him with your handbag?'

He, of course, did not understand a word I said.

'Let's go,' he shouted. 'One more time!' Another dive, another pull-up.

'Maybe you should take up some other line of work,' I said, 'or maybe you're hoping Orca will laugh himself to death.'

Angelica, writhing in terror against her chain, chose this moment to assert her religious affiliation.

'Hear, oh Israel!' she cried. 'The Lord our God, the Lord is one! Mayday! Mayday! Mayday!'

'You're a day late and a shekel short with Jehovah,' I shouted to her. 'Now we're stuck with Ariosto.'

'Yeah, right!' she shouted back. 'Is somebody going to rescue me or what? Right now Orca seems to be ahead on points.'

After a few more tries Ruggiero abandoned his Orca-killing charade and we swooped down for him to unchain Angelica and airlift her to safety, thus saving her life while imperilling her chastity. As we did so there came to me some half-memory of a legendary ring.

'Keep your eye on her ring,' I said as Ruggiero put Angelica on my pillion seat and we took off. As always he understood not a word.

Enjoying the weight of her sweet buttocks on my back I resigned myself to whatever disappointment was coming next. Ruggiero's mind was an easy one to read – he mostly had one thing on it. As Angelica clasped him from behind he could feel the heat of her breasts right through his armour and he was confident of claiming his reward for the rescue. As soon as he descried a suitable landing spot he put us down and began to struggle out of his armour, somewhat impeded by his erection. Cursing and sweating, inspired by Angelica's nakedness and maddened by his heroic tumescence he strove to make himself available for the longed-for embrace.

The ring? It was still in my mind but there was nothing I could do to prevent what would happen next. I could see Angelica waiting in fear and trembling for Ruggiero's onslaught but then she looked at her hand and there it was, the golden ring to break all spells and render its wearer invisible. Immediately she put it in her mouth and disappeared from view.

Ruggiero's frustration was nothing to me but how was *I* to find her again? With my animal sense of smell I detected her fragrance lingering on the air, compounded with the salt-sea tang and the sharp scent of her fear. But she was for the present lost to me and I was in myself confused and lost; Ariosto's words had left me!

I was aloft but without focus and direction. Why did I not fall? Something was sustaining me, but what? On the screen of my mind there flickered, like summer lightning, scenes of battle and courtship, chivalry and treachery, life and death in rapidly changing colours, and with them came, as from a great distance, their sounds. I understood then that the story, not only of Ariosto but of Angelica and me, had moved away from me. I flew in aimless circles, asking questions of the air that gave no answers. I had broken rules not allowed to be broken; what new rules was I now bound by?

Angelica Greenberg who is also Ariosto's Angelica, you and I belong together; there is a mystery between us; I must find you!

15

Yesterday's Seguidillas

On the screen of my mind there flicker, like summer lightning, scenes of battle and courtship, chivalry and treachery, life and death in rapidly changing colours, and with them come, as from a great distance, their sounds.

Here am I, Angelica Greenberg of San Francisco, but at the same time I am Ariosto's Angelica who was chained to a rock to await Orca's pleasure. Shall I always be this double Angelica? I am for the present out of the action as the story moves elsewhere.

There is a golden ring in my mouth. I put it on my finger and consider what to do next. I am in a clearing in a wood. There is a stream. I don't want to go anywhere in particular and I really don't want to do anything but think about Volatore, my imaginary lover who covered me as the griffin covered his mother. Bestiality. Why does my body thrill to the memory of it? I have had him as animal and I could have him as man but I can't have him as both at once. Not only does my body crave him but my soul also; that's the mystery of it and I am chained to that mystery as I was to my rock.

I know that he longs for me as I long for him. Obviously we've been dropped from Ariosto's story. What about our own story? We weren't meant to *have* our own story, is that it? Against the rules evidently. So where does that leave us?

My mind turned to my fifteen-years-gone father, and on impulse I rang up the KDFC *Morning Show* and got Hoyt Smith.

'Good morning!' he said. 'How's this day looking where you are?'

'Backward.'

'At?'

'The past.'

'"The past is a foreign country: they do things differently there."'

'Don't they just.'

'Where in the present are you calling from?'

'The Eidolon Gallery.'

'That's where there was a show with nudes on Harley Davidsons, right?'

'Right. Ossip Przewalski.'

'His paintings stay in the mind.'

'Yes, and naked women have been moving off the shelves like hotcakes.'

'I could talk to you all day but the clock is telling me to move on. What's your pleasure?'

'Would you play the "*Va, pensiero*" chorus from *Nabucco*?'

'Gladly.'

'From Carmencita.'

'To?'

'Whoever's listening.'

'Now for a little Rossini: "*Una voce poco fa*" from *Il barbiere di Siviglia* with Maria . . .'

I switched off. I know it was callas of me but I wasn't in the mood for anything that light-hearted. I had left my number and Smith promised to phone me to say when *Nabucco*'s Greenbergs would be hanging their harps on the airwaves.

Thinking my thoughts I drifted through the morning with nothing much doing at the gallery but wandering lookers who didn't know their ass from third base. In the afternoon I set off for my weekly session with Professor Beard. Not my idea. I had told my doctor, Dr Sugarman, that personal problems were getting me down and he referred me to Beard.

'He's English,' he said. 'Very advanced. He studied with Karl Kleinkopf who had his analysis with Wilhelm Gutschnerz who had his with Sigmund Freud.'

From what I'd heard, the last time Freud was at the cutting edge of shrinkage was back when Model Ts were rolling off Henry Ford's assembly line. But I didn't want to disillusion Doc Sugarman so I said OK I'd give Beard a try. Which is why I found myself watching the beardless

Prof Beard's prominent Adam's apple rise and fall as he spoke. Beard had a weak chin, rimless glasses, no wings.

'And when did you last see your father, heh heh?' said the (no) Beard.

'Why the heh heh?' I said.

'Nervous tic, ignore it. When did you?'

'Last see my father? When I was fifteen, the day before he took off with a lap dancer.'

'A dancer from Lapland? Where did he find her?'

'In his lap, where else? What's this got to do with my reality problems?'

'I have in mind your fascination with sexual intercourse with animals.'

'Only my hippogriff, and he's imaginary.'

'Quite: an imaginative displacement of your sexual longings for your father,' said the Prof. 'We've talked about this.'

'*You* have,' I said, 'but you're barking up the wrong tree.'

'Which tree would you suggest?'

By then I was no longer listening.

'Carmencita', my father used to call me, 'Zingarachen' and 'My little gypsy'. He loved opera and his favourite was *Carmen*. He had an album with Agnes Baltsa in the title role and when Mom got sick of hearing it – he always played it so the windows rattled – she threw it out, knowing he'd know he hadn't lost it but ready to charge him with making it disappear if he said he couldn't find it. There were tottering stacks of LPs and books in the studio; he had no indexing system, plus treacherous hands that *did* make things disappear. Regularly. About a third of his working time was spent in searching through the tottering stacks for the urgently needed opera, cantata or book, with cursing, whimpering and shouting. Then he'd buy again the lost treasure. He never lost *Carmen* though, always kept it on top of the opera stack. He knew Mom had thrown it out so he bought another one that cost three times as much as the one the garbage men had taken away. It was a recognised form of warfare between the two of them and they both knew the rules of engagement.

'Listen to that mezzo,' he would say. 'It's like silk but Baltsa puts a razor edge on it when the scene calls for it. If I could draw and paint the way she sings I'd draw and paint much better than I do.' And he'd sing the seguidilla off-key:

> "*Près des remparts de Seville,
> Chez mon ami Lillas Pastia . . .*"

and dance me around with a lot of stamping and a rose in the buttonhole of his shirt if one was available. While Mom ran the vacuum cleaner to drown out the noise. So they each got some satisfaction.

Dad took nothing with him when he left, so I ended up with the tottering stacks. I listened through the operas and indexed them. It was nothing from *Carmen* that attached itself to my AWOL father, but the famous chorus from *Nabucco*, '*Va, pensiero* . . .' 'Fly, thought, on wings of gold . . .' as the Jews, all of them named Greenberg, were led away into captivity. By the rivers of Babylon, there we sat down, yea, we wept when we remembered Zion. We hanged our harps upon the willows and tried to figure out whose fault it was.

'Shit happens,' said my best friend Rosie Margolis. 'It's called a mid-life crisis. My dad did the same thing.'

'Lap dancer?' It was Rosie's mother who had reported the breaking news of Dad's *Entführung* from the domestic hearth.

'Stuntwoman. Mom says he'll need a stunt*man* for the action scenes.'

'*My* mom says she's wasted a lot of years on Dad and now she's out for a good time.'

'Grown-ups!' said Rosie, and we both shook our heads. 'By the way,' she said, 'your dad's lap dancer is working her way through college; she's doing art history at UCLA.'

'It's good that she has something besides her ass to fall back on,' I said while wishing her dead.

The whole thing was hard for me to take in, and it came to me then — though I ought to have known it at fifteen — that parents, especially fathers, were not to be trusted, however reliable they might seem.

Mom was a painter who exhibited at the Eidolon Gallery under her maiden name, Lydia Katz. She looked enough like Agnes Baltsa to be her sister; if she'd been a singer she'd have been a mezzo and a fiery Carmen. Her paintings, however, were gentle and sunny, reminiscent of Bonnard. She'd met Dad at Friday-night life classes at the Sketch Club.

He was – still is, I hope – a big man with a shambling walk, several days' growth of beard and a funky man-smell that made me feel cosy and safe when I sat in his lap with his Old No. 7 Tennessee Sour Mash Whiskey breath warm on my neck and his stubble scraping my cheek as he read to me such favourites as Lear's tragedy of the Yonghy-Bonghy-Bo and his rejection by the Lady Jingly Jones:

> Though you've such a tiny body
>   And your head so large doth grow;
>   Though your hat may blow away,
>   Mr Yonghy-Bonghy-Bo!
> Though you're such a Hoddy Doddy
> Yet I wish that I could modify
>   the words I needs must say!
>   Will you please to go away? . . .

Sometimes late at night I'd hear sounds on the other side of the wall and I'd put a pillow over my head.

'Which tree would you suggest?' someone was saying. Beard?

'Please do your tree association in your own time,' I said. 'I asked you to check out *Orlando Furioso*. Have you?'

'My dear Ms Greenberg, my reading time is pretty well taken up with professional journals.'

'Look, Prof, I was referred to you by my doctor because I was getting headaches from the stress of my personal problems.'

'Which are, specifically?'

'I'm trying, for Christ's sake, to deal with two kinds of reality.'

'Right there is where your trouble is. There's only one reality – anything else is all in your head.'

'We're going in circles, Prof. I think I might have to take my business elsewhere, like Clancy's Bar.'

'You're of course free to terminate the therapy at any time. Sleep on it and let my secretary know at least twenty-four hours before your next session.'

'OK, Professor Beard. See you. Or not.'

I left his office humming the seguidilla with lots of foot-stamping in my head.

16

For Whom the Bell Clangs

It clanged for me as the car made its stops and starts on the way to Clancy's, tolling out the years of my growing up. All in a jangle of tintinnabulation: Dad gone; Berkeley; Michael; Mom's death. She'd boasted of being out for a good time but without the constant excitement of her ongoing war with Dad the future was too much for her to swallow and she got cancer of the oesophagus. So why did I buy the gallery? Why do people climb mountains of guilt, cross deserts of regret and travel long roads of too-late to give to the dead the love they couldn't give the living? Because that's what people do. While Dad was there Mom was just somebody at the other end of the table; my childhood scrapes and bruises were for Dad to kiss better and my report cards for him to admire. Lydia Katz continues to sell well: her paintings look good on any wall and she's a lot cheaper than Bonnard.

I have always kept a journal, and at college I did a writing course and was told by Oscar Glock, who taught the course, that I had talent. He was not, however, terribly impressed by talent.

'Talent,' he said, 'is cheap. The woods are full of talented people who will never do doodly-shit because they haven't got the *cojones* to go in over the horns.'

Mr Glock was given to bullfighting and boxing metaphors. He was shorter than Hemingway but he had a full Hemingway beard and he had published a novel called *Suit of Lights*.

The gallery leaves me plenty of time for writing and I may very well have the *cojones* but I've not yet found the right horns to go in over. Of course my imaginary animal friend keeps me pretty busy one way and another but once I get my head sorted I'll be better organised. Probably.

17

From Verse to Bad

It was the middle of a Thursday morning, so there was less of a crush than usual and Himself was sitting at a corner table reading *Orlando Furioso* with a coffee at his elbow while Javier tended bar.

Clancy Yeats is about forty, ten years older than I am. He's a big man who could be described as ruggedly handsome. He looks a bit like an actor whose name I don't remember, the one who often plays the male lead's best friend who doesn't get the girl. He came to SF from County Antrim a while back on a visit and stayed on. He inherited enough money to buy the bar and here he is. His wife left him three years ago and now he's divorced and has a teenage daughter he rarely sees. The last I heard she was living in Rome with her art teacher.

'Hi, Angie,' he said. 'I'm glad you recommended this. Ariosto's a real page-turner. His heroes and their journeys far/All come to life here in this bar,/With beauties needing to be saved/And many dangers to be braved.'

'It's catching,' I said. 'Those tales of his that I have read/Have made big trouble in my head:/I don't know if I'm here or there/or drifting somewhere in the air.'

'Tell me what the problem is,' said Clancy. 'That's what I'm here for. The tables and the chairs and the bar are just a front.'

'Have you done Canto Eye Vee yet?' (I always speak Roman numerals as their alphabet letters.) 'The part where the hippogriff is described?'

'I have that.'

'Does he seem real to you?'

'Yes, in the same way as selkies or werewolves. Maybe you should have a drink, just to settle the dust.'

'You're right as always, Clance. Let me have a Peroni and a double Laphroaig.'

'A boilermaker on an empty stomach: I'm assuming you've had no lunch.'

'Right again. Maybe Charlie can do me a steak sandwich.'

Charlie, who was lounging in a chair by the window, waved to me and fired up his grill. He was a taciturn man with a hoarse voice and he looked piratical, always with a kerchief round his throat.

'All right, Angie. Tell me about the hippogriff.'

'His name is Volatore.'

'I didn't see that in the book.'

'It's not in the book.'

'Then where'd you find it? Google? Wikipedia?'

'He told me it.'

'Ah! You haven't a drop taken already, have you?' His head a little bit on one side as he looked at me. Askance.

'Cold sober, Clance. Scout's honour.'

'What were you on when he told you?'

'Only a little Laphroaig to steady my nerves – not enough to get me drunk.'

'Where were you at the time?'

'In my apartment. I had Monteverdi on the Bose, Emma Kirkby singing "Olimpia's Lament". The music lifted him up to my window.'

I could feel that first encounter with Volatore becoming huge in me, wanting to burst like a watermelon dropped from a tenth-storey window. I knew I'd be sorry but I couldn't stop.

'You were saying?' said Clancy.

'I asked him in for a cup of tea.'

'How'd he get in?'

'Through the window.'

'And him quite a big fellow with hooves and talons and wings and all.'

'He thought small.'

Charlie brought my sandwich over and I sipped my beer.

Clancy waited until I had somewhat appeased my hunger and my thirst.

'I'm all ears,' he said then, looking prescient.

'I gave him tea in a bowl, because of his beak.'

'As one would. Go on.'

'I don't know what came over me . . .'

'Take your time, choose your words carefully.'

'I wanted him to kiss me.'

'Not a very soft kisser, with that beak.'

'He offered to change to a man-shape, but I told him I wanted him as he was.'

'Wanted him as in "I *want* you"?'

'Yes.'

'Hang on a moment,' said Clancy.

He went to the bar, came back with a bottle of Bushmill's and a glass, poured himself a stiff one, drank it down, and while catching his breath indicated to me that I should continue.

'Well of course he was too big for me so I asked him to think himself and his business smaller.'

Why was I telling Clancy all this? Did I want to make it irrevocably real by reliving it before him? Did I want to word myself naked under a beast to excite him and myself? Was I compelled by some inner demon to commit this act of betrayal? Yes to all of the above as I continued, 'And when the size was right I . . .'

'You don't have to say it all out.'

'Yes, I do because we're talking about a reality that's not the usual thing. I was only wearing panties and a bra so I took those off and got down on all fours and he covered me the way his father the griffin had covered his mother the mare.'

'His mother the mare . . .' He lingered over the words. 'How long ago was this?'

'I don't know what kind of time we're talking about.'

'What I mean is, did he make you pregnant?'

'Not in any way that ends up in the maternity ward.'

'What other kind of pregnant is there?'

'Mental, Clancy. All in the mind.'

'Leave any marks on you? I'd think his talons . . . unless they were all in the mind too.'

'There were some scratch marks but they've faded by now so I can't show you any evidence. Do you not believe me?'

A pause while Clancy Bushmilled himself again and I went on to my second boilermaker. The light through the window was very golden, and otherwise full of memories forgotten and remembered and there came to mind a Latin phrase from a book by Mircea Eliade, '*in illo tempore*', 'in that time'.

'I believe you, Ange – it's just that I don't know how to get my head around this other reality. I keep seeing you naked on all fours and him on top of you . . .' He trailed off into silence and he was blushing.

'Does it excite you?' I said.

'Yes.'

'Me too.'

Nobody said anything for a moment while the tourist influx murmured and drank its drinks. Then we looked at each other, nodded, and went upstairs.

When we had our clothes off Clancy blushed again and I read his mind.

I got down on all fours and said softly, 'Here I am. Take me.'

Afterwards, lying in his arms, I saw that he was crying.

'What is it, Clance?' I said, and kissed him.

'I can't describe it exactly,' he said. 'There's a great sadness come over me, what a little short thing it is to be alive and so strange. Maybe it's just the whisky.'

'No, it's the sense of loss, something lost so far back we can't remember it.'

'Were you thinking of Volatore while we were doing it?'

'Yes.'

'Was it better with him? Did it give you that thing that was lost so far back?'

'I don't want to talk about it, Clance. It was what it was.'

'And you're hugging the memory to yourself, not to lose the goodness of it, yes?'

'Please, Clancy!'

'What happened after he climbed off you? Did you fly away together?' His face as he said that was not the face of anyone I wanted to be with and I felt thoroughly ashamed, as I had known all along I would be.

'That's as far as this conversation goes,' I said.

I got dressed while he watched me in a dirty-minded way, and left.

'Come back soon,' he called to my departing back. 'You can be on top next time.'

18

The Eight O'Clock to Katerini

There is a jukebox in my head. Coloured lights, bubbles going round into vanishment and reappearing to go round again. I have no choice in what songs are played. Sometimes a lissom cheerleader inserts the coins, sometimes a tattooed truck driver; the mystic arm rises and descends with the silent disc which then blossoms into song and I dance or cry or shake my head accordingly.

This time it is a woman in black who feeds the Wurlitzer. The mystic arm rises, descends, and an empty railway station arises in the November evening around Agnes Baltsa as she sings in her native Greek '"*To treno fevgi stis okto*" ', 'The train leaves at eight'. The woman in black remembers, will never forget the eight o'clock to Katerini and a lost love. This is not Baltsa wearing the borrowed language of Bizet; here, giving her whole heart to this little story in the tongue she was born into, she sings me the empty platform, the gathering November night and the departure of love and I cry accordingly.

19

A Little Way on the Tin Globe

I phoned my partner Olivia to tell her that I'd not be at the gallery that day, and I went to the overlook at Fort Point to sit and think about things. The sky was blue, the sunlight danced on the water, ships and boats came and went. Round and round in my mind went this time, that time, all time. *In illo tempore.* My childhood. Telling the bees. My grand-mother told me about that. Her husband had joined the International Brigade in 1936 and went off to the Spanish Civil War. Sometimes when she and I were alone and she'd had too much to drink she'd talk about that time.

'He said it was something he had to do,' she said. 'I told him there were things he had to do right here, like fix the hole in the roof of the barn. He did it and then he went off to fight fascism.'

She was a good-looking old woman in a plough-that-broke-the-plains kind of way but her face became almost girlish as she called up the past.

'Those days seem a long way back,' she said. 'The images were brighter, the smells and flavours stronger than now: the taste of honey in the comb, the smell of it and the feel of the wax on my tongue, the stickiness all around my mouth and on my fingers. Sweet, like the golden time that passes; the pink apple blossoms drifting down on the hives in the summer orchard.

'Before he left he told me to tell the bees. "Be very careful to say that I've just gone away for a while but I'm not dead. If they think I'm dead they'll leave our hives and swarm somewhere else."

'"You're very superstitious all of a sudden," I said to him.

'"Traditions matter," he said, "and bees are very serious people."

'We had a tin globe on the desk where we did the accounts,' said my grandmother. 'On it Spain was only a little way from North America but on the real globe it was a world away from Bakersfield where we lived then. I tried to imagine that war but I couldn't, it was a whole different reality.' Her face looked so young!

'I told the bees and they stayed with us until the summer of 1938. I saw them swarm away out of the orchard and I cried a lot but we heard nothing until a year later when one of his comrades sent us a letter saying that my man had died at a place called Teruel. I couldn't find it on the globe but it was in the big atlas.

'There was a plaster bust of Lenin on top of the grand-father clock in the front room. I was dusting it when we got the letter and I knocked it on to the floor where it smashed into smithereens. "Well," I said, "I guess it was your time to go."'

Why does her story come to me so vividly now? Back when she told it I had never heard of a hippogriff. What's the connection? Then it rises like a golden carp glimmering. The bees. They existed in their time and space in our orchard but they partook of that other time and space where men with bolt-action rifles were saving the world. Telling the bees was folklore but it worked with real bees.

Two kinds of reality – it happens.

20

Home Thoughts from Aloft

I began to dream of Volatore. Always we were flying in a greyness. Not like fog but the absence of everything. I felt the heat of his body between my bare legs and the rhythmic tensing of his great wing muscles but there was no sound. I looked for a rift in the silence and the greyness through which I might see the world but there was none.

I said, 'I don't think we're getting anywhere.'

No answer and the silence woke me up.

It was true enough that we weren't getting anywhere but I could feel that the connection between us was unbroken. And Volatore was still flying, I was sure of that. Lost perhaps and lonely but still flying. Think of me, Volatore! Think of your Angelica!

21

In Loco Wyatt Earpis

With the stress of two realities, one of which was not officially allowed to non-crazies, my head was badly in need of reorganisation. I didn't think I was crazy but I wasn't too sure of my sanity. I had abandoned Professor Beard and I was with a new psychotherapist, recommended by Olivia, Dr Levy. He was short, bald, wore very thick glasses and a Wyatt Earp moustache.

'So,' he said, 'what's the problem?'

'I seem to be living in two kinds of reality,' I said. 'Two kinds of time. Do you know what a hippogriff is?'

'Yes, it's an imaginary animal.'

'Well, I have a kind of relationship with one.'

'Sexual?'

'Yes.'

'Do you dream about him?'

'Yes.'

'What are you doing in the dream?'

'Sitting on his back while we fly through a greyness.'

'To where?'

'Nowhere, I told him that we weren't getting anywhere.'

'Is your father alive?'

'I don't know. I haven't heard from him for a long time and I don't know where he is.'

'Do you miss him?'

'Sometimes.'

'This hippogriff may very well be a displacement of sexual longings for your father. Have you read my comparative study of the Ghost Dance and the Cargo Cults?'

He took a book with that title off his desk and thrust it into my hands. On the back cover was a large photograph of him dressed more or less like Wyatt Earp.

'No,' I said. 'What have the Ghost Dance and the Cargo Cults to do with me?'

'Imaginative displacement and believing that wishing will make it so.'

He looked at his watch, wrote a prescription and gave it to me.

'What's this?' I said.

'It's a placebo, extra-strength. Take two with water as required.'

'But a placebo's all in the mind. The word is the Latin for "I shall please". If you think it'll work, it will.'

'There you go. Get my secretary to book a session for you for next week.'

Is there a placebo effect, I wondered, for 'Everything is OK'? So if you think it is, it is? I tried it but I didn't really think it was and it wasn't.

22

Volatore's Ghost Dance

What? Where? No, how? How is this that I am . . . what?
A ghost? A revenant? I was Volatore, yes? So what am I
now? The ghost of myself? No, this is really too much!
To be the ghost of an imaginary self! If indeed I am a
ghost I am not one of those who clanks his chains, no! I
dance with rage!

23

Isaiah's Ghost Dance

Dr Levy had compared my 'imaginative displacement' to the Ghost Dance of the Southwest Indians. My curiosity was piqued but instead of reading his book I went to Google, which took me to the massacre at Wounded Knee. I cry easily, and I wept as I read the words and images on my computer screen. To this small excitation of phosphors have the Sioux warriors of the plains come at last!

I was still at the office computer when I saw two figures at the gallery doors. By their in-your-face humble posture I recognised them as Jehovah's Witnesses and went to meet them. One was a young woman, the other a middle-aged man. The woman was modestly frumped-up but she was pretty in a way that made me think her name might have been Tiffany or Amber before she went into the witnessing business. The man had painfully sincere horn-rimmed glasses and grey hair.

'Hello,' said the woman. 'My name is Ruth and this is my father Jonathan.'

'How do you do,' I said.

We shook hands.

'We've been going around,' said Ruthany, 'asking folks how they feel about the world today. Would you say you feel optimistic about it?'

'Definitely pessimistic,' I said.

'Many people tell us that,' she assured me without placing a hand on my arm, 'and Scripture gives us an answer in Isaiah, Chapter 65, Verse 17.' Her fast-draw Bible appeared open in her hands before my reply had cleared the holster.

I read, 'For, behold, I create new heavens and a new earth: and the former shall not be remembered, nor come into mind.'

'But that's imaginative displacement,' I said, 'and believing that wishing will make it so. It's a Ghost Dance!'

'Say what?' said Ruthany.

'Wovoka, the Paiute holy man from Nebraska, in 1888 had a vision during a solar eclipse, and he started the Ghost Dance Religion.' I read off my computer printout: ' "He claimed that the earth would soon perish and then come alive again in a pure, aboriginal state, replete with lush green prairie grass, large buffalo herds and Indian ancestors."

'He told the Indians how to earn this new reality, with prayer and meditation and especially dancing "through which one might briefly die and catch a glimpse of the Paradise to come".

'The government banned the Ghost Dance, the Indians didn't stop, so on the morning of 29 December 1890, at Wounded Knee, the soldiers killed a hundred and fifty Indians and wounded fifty, all of them wearing Ghost Shirts to stop the bullets.' By this time I was crying again.

'She's upset,' said Jonathan to Ruth. 'We'll talk about this another time,' he said to me as I sat there in my Ghost Shirt, weeping by the rivers of Babylon.

24

Pictures in the Sand

Sometimes I listen to gospel songs. I like the way they sound. There's one called 'Far Side Bank of Jordan' in the Alison Krauss and the Cox Family album, *I Know Who Holds Tomorrow*. Willard Cox sings of leaving this world before his wife and waiting for her by the River Jordan while drawing pictures in the sand.

Listening to that song I see, beyond the Jordan, vast herds of buffalo grazing on the lush green grass. And I see the tents of the ancestors and the smoke of their fires. Frying fish from the Jordan, maybe. Rainbow trout, big ones.

25

Broad-Mindedness of Volatore

Angelica, no word for me? After all that has passed between us! Are you perhaps now having doubts because you're a Jewess and my literary father Ariosto was a Catholic? But love knows no barriers – ethnic differences are nothing to me – both of my birth parents almost certainly worshipped the old gods, as do I. Put aside your doubts – there are no religious obstacles to our union!

26

Dim Red Taverns of Sheep

Hoyt Smith rang me up to tell me that my request would go out next morning between eleven and twelve. While waiting for that to happen I acted on a heads-up from Phyllis Stein. She collects the paintings and drawings of autistic savants in the belief that they contain hidden messages. She said there was a fellow in Hunter's Point who was doing the Periodic Table of the Elements with nude figures in elemental combinations, explicitly. Sadominsky was his name and she wanted me to check him out before she showed her chequebook.

So I schlepped myself out to the address she gave me, an ex-factory of some kind, all girders and skylights and high spaces. The door was open and as I stepped inside the Smell hit me. Yes, *that* one: Volatore! Holding myself ready for whatever there was to be ready for, I advanced slowly.

'Well,' said a husky voice with a heavy accent, 'you looking for?'

'Sadominsky?' I said as I described a bulky figure in a shadowy corner.

'Zhabotinsky am.'

'Oh, sorry.'

'Who sent?'

'Me?'

'Why?'

'Aren't you doing the Periodic Table of the Elements with nude figures?'

'They say I?'

'You what?'

'Automatic?'

'You mean autistic?'

'Not am. Eccentric, OK? They always.'

'Get it wrong?'

'Not Periodic Table.'

'Not?'

'Big not. Beeriodic Fable of the Elephants.'

'Elephants!'

'With beer tell fable to.'

'Whom?'

The smell got stronger as he put his head on one side and looked at me slyly.

'Winey, winey trancing clients in the dim red taverns of sheep.'

'Sheep!'

'Baa.'

'Who are you?'

'Zhabotinsky.'

'Your name's always been Zhabotinsky?'

'Only since born. See paintings?'

'All right, let's see them.'

We went past his kitchen to get to the paintings. It consisted of the factory sink, a little fridge, a Coleman stove, and a cardboard box for crockery and pots and pans. Some beets in a string bag. The furniture was orange crates. No empty pizza or Chinese cartons, his budget clearly didn't run to such luxuries. His clothes were shabby and he was pretty scruffy. The guy was poor.

There were lots of canvases: he was a full-time painter, so what was Volatore to him or he to Volatore? The smell, I noticed, was gone. The paintings were weird and witty and original, not like anyone else's.

'These are very good,' I said.

'Talk numbers?' he said.

'Big numbers if I can sell you as an autistic savant.'

'No prob. Big autistic savant, me.'

He probably hadn't ever sold a picture before. He was a latter-day Albert Pinkham Ryder, a recluse who had uncashed cheques lying around all over the place. Except this one had no cheques, maybe he lived on an allowance from an older brother in Siberia, who knows. Maybe he was a dishwasher in some café. Certainly no part of any artistic community or he'd have learned the ropes and found some buyers. A dyed-in-the-wool loner. I was pretty sure I could do right by him.

'Phone?' I said.

He took one out of his pocket; he was at least that much connected to the age of technology and commerce.

'Got a first name?' I asked him.

'Alexander. Alyosha you can.'

'Call you. OK, Alyosha. Let's see if we can move you into a higher income bracket.' I wrote down his cell-phone number and said, 'I'll phone you tomorrow or the day after and arrange to bring somebody to see your work. Be careful crossing streets and don't talk to strangers. *Do svidaniya.*'

He kissed my hand. Blessed are the pure in heart, but it takes more than purity to put blintzes on the table.

But Volatore! My Volatore was trying to reach me! Yes,

> One day soon, you and I will merge,
> Everything that rises must converge . . .

Yes, my love! I want to merge with you, I long for the two of us to converge! Was it you who put a coin in my jukebox to play me that old Shriekback track? Clever Volatore!

27

Cigarettes and Heart Trouble

I switched on KDFC a little before eleven just to be on the safe side. 'Carmencita,' Smith was saying, 'which has put me in the mood for Georges Bizet's masterpiece. *Carmen* is one of those classics every mezzo has to face. Year after year they step up to the plate to see if they can knock it out of the park. Most of them get a base hit but not too many put a home run up on the scoreboard. You're about to hear one who who belts it like the old Bambino, Babe Ruth himself. Elina Garanca truly does the biz for Bizet: Carmen sings the seguidilla seated in a chair with her hands tied behind her back. She's knifed another girl at the cigarette factory where they both work and now, under arrest, she is alone with Don José, the dragoon corporal guarding her while she waits to go to prison. Carmen methodically sets out to seduce him, he unties her hands and she's off like a shot to join her smuggler pals at Lillas Pastia's tavern.

'Garanca's mezzo can do anything and her Carmen could have seduced the whole platoon, let alone a mama's boy like Don José.'

'"*Près des remparts de Seville,*"' she sings,

> '"*Chez mon ami Lillas Pastia.*
> *Nous dansons la seguidille*
> *Et boirons du Manzanilla.*
> *Tra la la la la la!*"'

Her voice transported me to that time, *illo tempore*, when my father and I danced our seguidilla in the foreign country that is the past. '"*Va, pensiero!*"' I sang, and listened for the Babylon-river Greenbergs to join me. But Hoyt Smith was gone and I was hearing the news, I had missed my message to whoever was listening.

28

Pheromonal

Lydia Greenberg, née Katz, had a brother. Leo, who is still with us and in good health, had a daughter, Phyllis, who is Mrs Irving Stein. Mr Stein is rated by *Forbes* one of the ten richest men in America. He built his fortune from the bottom up by patenting and marketing the Stein EZ–Sit, an 'intimate-size' ring cushion that is worn inside (loose-fitting) clothes and eases the discomfort of haemorrhoids and other afflictions of the down-belows.

Phyllis Stein, probably around forty, give or take, rejoices in a figure both firm and compact, and her face isn't too bad when she stops frowning and puts on her glasses. She keeps *The Kama Sutra* and her vibrator under her silk undies in the Fornasetti chest of drawers in her separate bedroom.

Although she has never performed, she has studied modern dance with a teacher who studied modern dance under Martha Graham. As Phyllis moves about the house she does Martha Graham contractions while making little tongue-clickings that irritate her white-haired husband who walks with an ebony-and-ivory stick that cost more than the cook earns in six months.

'If you've got stomach cramps why don't you take something for it?' he rasps, pausing for a fit of coughing.

Phyllis ignores him while wishing she had a house savant who could give her a good clear estimate on how soon she might expect to wear the black Versace (waiting in the Fornasetti) of her grieving widowhood. A short course of too much sex might send Irving out of this vale of tears like laundry down a chute but it's been a long time since Irving was up to even minimal slap-and-tickle, and as yet Phyllis has no Plan B.

What about the hidden messages in her collection of drawings and paintings by autistic savants? Forget it. Concentrating on them until her eyes bulge out of her head and her brain is pulsing like a jellyfish, she can extract nothing from them but squadrons of meaningless numbers and drifts of recondite architectural detail.

So, when Angelica phones, a little trickle of saliva runs down Phyllis's chin, and Chow Yun Thin, her driver, is holding open the door of the raspberry-ripple Lamborghini before you can say Chow Yun Fat. He puts the pedal to the medal, and as streets and houses and her life flash by she feels the fickle finger of Fate doing the right thing for once and she senses that this day is not going to be like other days.

Arrived at the girders and skylights and high places, she is drawn, like iron filings to a magnet, to the shadowy corner from which issues the Siberian bass of Alexander Zhabotinsky.

'You have,' he bellows softly.

'Come,' she breathes.

'Big autist me,' he says. 'Vroom. Four on the.'

'Floor, dear,' sighs Phyllis as Angelica and Chow Yun Thin retire to the kitchen where Angelica fills two cracked mugs with tea from her flask.

Among the canvases, Phyllis and Alyosha crouch close enough together to inhale each other's pheromones as he guides her through *The Beeriodic Fable of the Elephants*. Phyllis is by now realising that she is smelling the hidden message she has been seeking. It is large and shabby and scruffy and its name is Alyosha. She needs some adjectives to fill out that name, and must get a Russian dictionary.

So, breathing in and out in sync, with Phyllis's cheque-book wet with anticipation, these two recede from view, leaving us to reflect that the *Drang nach Osten* is a faster pull than it used to be. Maybe it's the global warming.

29

Lap of Honour

All of a sudden there he was. Dad, on the outside looking in through the glass doors of the gallery. I went to meet him with the ache in my throat predicting tears. I opened the door and he came in hesitantly.

'Would you like to hug me?' I said. 'There's a small charge but you can run a tab.'

We hugged, I inhaled the Dad plus Old No. 7 Tennessee Sour Mash Whiskey smell, we cried a little, wiped our tears, blew our noses, stepped back and looked at each other. He wasn't in bad shape for a fifty-nine-year-old unshaven type. White hair, some wear and tear but not too much. We hugged again, stepped back again.

'Carmencita,' he said, and kissed the top of my head.

'Did you listen to my request?' I asked him.

'My name is Whoever.'

'Before "*Va, pensiero*" did you hear Garanca do the seguidilla?'

'Sure I did. That's some dynamite mezzo! I've just heard that she does *Carmen* on DVD and I'm definitely going to get it as soon as I can.'

'So has the train pulled out and left Agnes Baltsa on the empty station platform?'

'Later loves come along, but a first love is the one that took you to a place you never knew before, so it'll always be part of you.'

'Way to go, Dad. You're a classy guy.'

'Well, you know, a man is either a gentleman or he's something to put out with the garbage.'

'I've seen some of your graphic novels and they're very good – really I think they're your best work.'

'Thank you, Carmencita. It's a whole new quality market that's opened up. I'm so much in demand that I'm actually turning down work.'

'Good for you, Dad, and I'm glad to smell that it's keeping you in Jack Daniel's.'

'You know it! And that Tennessee Sour Mash keeps my hand steady.'

'So tell me, do you always listen for messages from me on the *Morning Show*?'

'Of course.'

'Why?'

'Why does a salmon swim upstream?'

'To get to the other side?'

'That's it, and here I am. Can you forgive me?'

'Yes, I can.'

'I wasn't sure you would.'

'For a long time I couldn't but now I'm fifteen years older than I was when you left and I've learned one or two things. Sometimes a demon drives us to do what everybody wants us not to do and even we ourselves might want not to do it but we'll do it anyhow. That's just how people are.'

'About my not very original mid-life crisis – the girl I went off with was working at the Crazy Horse . . .'

'They have lap dancers there?'

'Nikki wasn't a lap dancer. She danced nude in the Crazy Horse revues.'

'You went to the Crazy Horse?'

'No. I met her at City College, in front of the Rivera mural. She was doing a course in the history of art at UCLA. She was only twenty, she was pretty and she was very easy to be with.'

'You were forty-four at the time and not quite in the Sean Connery class of pulling power. Why do you think she fell into your lap, so to speak?'

'I struck up a conversation with her, she liked talking to me and one thing led to another.'

'Where is she now?'

'Moved in with her history of art lecturer.'

'Aren't they usually married?'

'Or divorced.' He'd begun to look around at the walls. 'Not a bad painter. Lydia. Not very original but not bad. And looking at that *Interior with Sleeping Cat*, you'd think butter wouldn't melt in that woman's mouth.'

'But cool she wasn't, your wife and my mom.'

'Definitely not. What's this with multicoloured numbers copulating, *Ah, Love, Let Us Be the Square Root of True or Something Other?*'

'My cousin Phyllis is unloading some of the older autisic savants in her collection.'

'And this with the nude on a motorcycle, *Harley No. 7.*'

'Ossip Przewalski, he's a steady seller. Where are you living these days?'

'Furnished apartment in the Mission. Very Edward Hopper.'

'Feel like a classic pizza at Marco's?'

'If you let it be my treat, Carmencita.'

'You got it, Pops.'

Olivia, who had stayed in the office to give us privacy, now emerged for introductions.

'Olivia Partridge,' I said, 'this is my dad, the infamous Herman Greenberg.'

'Famous too,' she said to Dad. 'Didn't you do *Worlds without Worlds*, words *and* pictures?'

'Yup,' said the graphically novel parent, shuffling his feet modestly. 'Lettering's the hardest part. Olivia, could you join us for pizza at Marco's?'

'I thought you'd never ask,' she said, blushing prettily while Dad admired her legs.

Off we went then, into a smiling spring evening, each of us wearing a smile.

30

Vroom Vroom

'Such wonderful pictures!' says Phyllis. 'And they're all done autistically?'

'New gearbox every time,' says Alyosha. 'Also valve job.'

'Take me through *The Beeriodic Fable of the Elephants* again, Alyosha. Here's the beginning of it, with an elephant dozing in a hammock slung between two trees.'

'Is Dimitri Pyotr Elephantovitch, ZZZZZZZ peacefully.'

'When suddenly . . .'

'Suddenly TSADSABAM!'

'Lightning strikes the tree WHAM!'

'Flaming fire bursting out SSWEEUUU!'

'But Dimitri Pyotr is ready for it.'

'With trunkful of beer squirting SSSSQUIRSHHH! Out goes fire tssss.'

'And the elephants tell this Beeriodic Fable to . . .'

'Elephant childs. Moral of fable: Always have trunkful of beer in case of stricken with lightning.'

'Why not water, Alyosha?'

'Is oral tradition, always beer.'

'Love that fable, Alyosha.'

'All elephant childs learn this. Now I make for you some borscht, yes?'

31

Ingress of Volatore

I want to reach Angelica and I don't know how to do it. I can only proceed by trial and error. It was in this way that I chanced upon the mind of Alexander Zhabotinsky. An interesting habitat in which the proprietor appeared riding through a jungle on the back of a painted and bejewelled elephant, reclining in a gilded howdah with an attractive woman who was wearing only a pair of horn-rimmed spectacles. Entertainment was provided by a band of orang-utans in Cossack dress backing a parrot in a sequinned gown who sang, in English, tangos from Finland.

The mahout in charge of the elephant was described in Zhabotinsky's thoughts as 'dirtified pubic and counting'. This was of little interest to me until that individual turned and revealed himself to be none other than Vassily Baby, brother to Alexander.

'Aha! Vassily Baby! Well met!' Slipping into the mind I found in his head along with a cloud of Stolichnaya, I saw a tall building on which the name Jarley Goode Ltd was inscribed on a brass plate at the entrance.

The name had a moneyed sound, so I flew to the financial district of San Francisco. There stood Jarley Goode Ltd, where Vassily Baby was employed as a certified public accountant. In his thoughts as he studied a database on his computer I found that he had promised his widowed mother to look after his unworldly younger brother. So here was the source of the miserable pittance that kept Alyosha in beets and potatoes.

Recalling what a tight squeeze it had been to get into Vassily's mind that first time I wondered why it was so easy this time. Was Vassily weaker now? Was I stronger? Drifting through the barren and dusty attic of his largely unused brain I realised that I was much the stronger one. Vassily had never been in love, while I, loving Angelica steadfastly through thick and thin, had acquired mental and spiritual muscle that took me through his feeble defences easily.

It is said that revenge is a dish best served cold. Mine had had plenty of time to cool and I was looking forward to a long-deferred feast. Hovering high above him, I watched him leave his office. He stopped at a nearby delicatessen, bought a sandwich and a six-pack of beer, took them to his Mercedes and, with me following, drove to the Fort Point parking spot I remembered from our last meeting. From there he walked to the overlook, taking with him Stolichnaya from the glove compartment, and sat

down to eat his sandwich and drink his beer while waiting, I suppose, for his next beautiful stranger, or possibly
hoping for a return engagement with Angelica.

Vassily waited and I waited, hovering high above him
while the evening opened to that time that always catches
in my throat; the sky was still light but the bridge lamps
had come on and those in the houses across the bay. I
descended to twenty feet above Vassily's head – I wanted
him to see me grow suddenly huge as I dropped on him
from that height.

'Vassily Baby,' I yelled down to him, 'here is Volatore!'

He looked up and screamed but I was on him like an
owl on a mouse and there was nothing he could do, my
talons had him pinned.

'Call of nature! Trousers down!' I commanded, expos-
ing his nether parts to the cool evening air while he
whimpered piteously.

Then I thought a little smaller but not too much,
and really gave him something to scream about when I
achieved ingress by that same passage from which he had
evicted me one evening not so long ago. He was moan-
ing, possibly not from pleasure, when I left him there and
flew away. Vassily could not have imagined a hippogriff
but Ariosto did, so an eventful evening was had by all.

32

Double or Nothing?

The doubleness, always the doubleness! And so little certainty. None, in fact. For the present I seemed not to be subject to Ariosto's words. Wait, I thought, as an almost-idea rose to the surface: a something, a what? The almost-idea of a key, an action, a repositioning of mind, a placing of myself in a new relation to my situation. The bitten biting? The doubled unifying? The lost finding? Hang on!

Orlando Furioso is fiction, right? Ludovico Ariosto made it up out of his head. OK, it's a classic. I'm not saying that I, Angelica Greenberg, can write a classic, but maybe I can invent my own story and live into it. Why not? Maybe even octave stanzas. Here goes:

Angelica, now from Ariosto freed,
Thinks of her Volatore, wandering far;
To find him is her first and foremost need,

To seek him underneath his guiding star.
She knows not what Dame Fortune has decreed;
She'll carry on, whate'er her chances are.

On the other hand:

Let me now bring my rhyming to a close
And what I have to say I'll say in prose.

Because looking for a rhyme can drag you away from where you want to go. So I'll start again by setting out my objective. Which is what? Well, I want to hook up with Volatore again.

I'll do a little Q and A:

Q: How do you want to hook up with him, on all fours?

A: Let's leave sex out of it for the moment, OK?

Q: So in what form do you want him, beast or human?

A: The problem is that when he's human he's someone else.

And when he's a beast he's not really a suitable lover. I mean, I couldn't take him home to meet my parents. If I had any parents at home.

Q: Did you think your love was going to break an enchantment and reveal him as a handsome prince?

A: Spare me your sarcasm, OK?

Q: In the past you've had Volatore as idea without
     visible form. Want to try that again?

A: It's too much like hearing voices in my head. I
     was able to do it for a little while but longer would
     drive me crazy. Besides, he's got to be available for
     that to work.

Let's back up a little. Why am I attracted to Volatore?
Attraction is too weak a word – I am drawn to him as the
ocean is drawn to the full moon. Why? Is it the animal of
me being pulled by the animal of him? Like Pangaea that
was one continent until the tectonic plates moved apart;
now sea turtles have in them the cellular memory that
drives them across the far, far ocean miles to the place
that once was whole. *In illo tempore*. Do I believe that
Volatore and I were once one? That we were parted so
that a sea of emptiness appeared between us? Yes, I think
I do believe that. I believe in the primal animalness of
all of us. I believe in the imagined reality of us coupled
with the ordinary reality. We walk on our hind legs and
wear clothes but in our being are the almost-remembered
selves that went naked and speechless on all fours.

With all due respect – not all that much, actually – I
think the Beards and the Levys of this world have no idea
how to come to grips with my problem(s). Maybe I'll
have to go it alone. All right then, I'll see what I can do
with the story of me by me. No Ariosto.

33

A Place for Everything?

At first there was just one place which was everyplace. One thing which was everything. One body which was everybody.

Later there was one thing which was two, one double thing, one thing with two parts. Then the two separated. They became two ones. They were Volatore and Angelica and sometimes they were together but mostly they weren't. Then they disappeared from each other. Each could feel the presence of the other somewhere, but where?

Angelica tried to send her thoughts to Volatore. She sent this: Volatore, come to me! If you can't come to me, talk to me however you can!

Then she waited.

I looked at the two of them in my mind: a woman and a hippogriff. What if the woman became a hippogriff? No,

I wouldn't like that. And if the hippogriff became a man he'd have to take over some human's body and there are too many problems with that.

I looked at the two of them side by side and shook my head sadly.

'That's all I can think of right now,' I said. 'I'll try again another time.'

At this point I decided to abandon story-writing and just carry on typing out the events of every day as they happened. Ariosto imagined Volatore; Volatore imagined me but I can't imagine how our story ends. Bad word: I don't like to think of an end to our story.

34

Some Kind of a Joke?

I settled back into my normal routine. I saw Dr Levy every week and took my extra-strength placebos when the stress was more than usual. I kept a simple journal, nothing more, and I tried to find a quiet place to put my head. I wasn't giving up on Volatore but I needed to pull back from the front line for a little rest and rehabilitation. Whenever Clancy phoned I made it clear that our friendship was on hold. I went to the gallery every day and pretended that there was nothing else going on in my life.

Funny, how the mind brings up sights and smells from childhood. There was a day in April when the air seemed heavy with the impending season and there came to me the pungent odour of skunk cabbage and the clerical visage of Jack-in-the-pulpit. There was an old woman down the road who was versed in 'herbs and simples'. I suppose the simple part of it was to do with simple cures. She was known to have helped Jane Wakeman get rid of her baby when she was three months gone. She used the Jack-in-the-pulpit seeds for divination and it was said that she could tell when people were going to die.

She grabbed me by the arm once and put her face close to mine. I was eleven at the time.

'Ever dream of flying?' she said.

'No,' I said.

'You will,' she hissed. She made an obscene gesture and went away cackling to herself.

Remembering her I recalled my flights, waking and dreaming, with Volatore, the heat of his body between my legs and the funky animal smell of him.

On this April day in 2008 a man came into the gallery with a very wide canvas, six feet or so, wrapped in brown paper. His clothes, all paint-smeared, were new: black jeans, blue denim shirt, Timberland boots. He seemed clean enough but there was a strong smell about him, a funky animal smell that I recognised.

'Why are you blushing?' said Olivia.

'I don't know, maybe it's early change of life.'

Hard to tell his age: forty maybe. He was tall, strongly built, clean-shaven. Odd expression on his face. High on something?

'Have you made an appointment for us to see this man?' I asked Olivia.

'No,' she said. 'I haven't.'

'Are you Angelica Greenberg?' said the man to me in a Tom Waits kind of voice. His English was all right but it sounded dubbed, as in a foreign film where the speaker's lips aren't shaping the English words you hear.

'How do you know my name?' I said.

'It came to mind.'

'Came to mind how? In a dream? In a Rolodex?'

'I don't know.'

'And how did you know to come here to the gallery?'

'This is where my feet brought me.'

'Oh really? And what's your name?'

'Volatore.'

I jumped back as if he'd grabbed me by the crotch.

'Is this some kind of a joke?' I said in a voice that was not my normal one.

He reared back and showed the whites of his eyes like a half-broke horse.

'What's wrong with my name?'

'Where'd you get it?'

'It came to me.'

'Is it your first name?'

'It's my only.'

'Who are your parents?'

'No family, there's just me.'

'Where do you live?'

'Around.'

'Have you exhibited anywhere?'

'No. Are you going to look at the painting?'

'OK, mystery man, unveil it.'

He tore off the brown paper and threw it on the floor. As he did so I caught a glimpse of a naked woman tattooed on his right wrist. Not the usual full-frontal thing but with the body slightly turned and the left arm raised. He removed a Michnik from a nearby easel and put up his painting.

Olivia and I stepped back to viewing distance. 'Has it got a title?' I said.

'*Tiny, Tiny Dancing Giants in the Dim Red Caverns of Sleep*,' he answered.

Olivia and I stood there taking it in. The thing was unsettling but hypnotic and difficult to turn away from. You wouldn't call it figurative but it wasn't abstract either. There was a lot of dimness and redness and the idea of the tiny, tiny dancing giants was perfectly clear but not spelled out. Looking at it made me woozy and I had to lean against a wall to keep from falling over. We mostly have music in the gallery and this afternoon it was the Emma Kirkby recording that had lifted Volatore to my window. '"*Voglio, voglio*,"' she sang to Anthony Rooley's lute. '"*Voglio morire*,"' she sang, and the tiny, tiny dancing giants danced silently in the dim red caverns of the wide canvas.

'Opera?' said the man who called himself Volatore.

'No,' I said. 'It's "Olimpia's Lament" when Bireno sails away and she's left on the beach.'

He gave me a measured leer.

'You ever get left on the beach?'

'Don't get smart with me,' I said, 'I've dealt with better leerers than you.'

'*Sorry!*'

'You know *Orlando Furioso*? Vivaldi did an opera with that title, based on Ariosto's epic poem.'

'It's got plenty of operatic situations, like Orlando's fury because he's got the hots for Angelica but she wants no part of him. Happened because they drank from different fountains, kind of thing goes on every day in opera land.'

'So you've read it.'

'Guess I must have, since it's in my head.'

I almost said that he didn't look like a reader of sixteenth-century epic poetry, but decided not to.

Pause.

'Well?' he said, watching me with a condescending smile on his face.

'Where's this painting coming from?' I said. 'I mean the idea.'

'A dream.'

'Can you say a little more about it?'

'Everything I had to say is up there on the canvas.'

'What else have you painted?' said Olivia.

'Nothing.'

'Can you leave it with us and come back tomorrow?' I said. 'We'd like to give this some thought.'

'OK.'

'There's a shower here that you can use,' said Olivia, 'if you want to freshen up.'

'I always smell like this,' he said. 'See you.' He walked over the brown paper on the floor and out of the door.

The painting was still doing its thing on the easel but neither of us wanted to look at it. His smell lingered awhile.

About five minutes after he left I said to him, 'Wait!'

'What?' said Olivia.

'Never mind. My reflexes aren't what they used to be.'

'What were you going to say to him?' said Olivia.

'I'm not sure.'

'His visit seems to have hit you kind of hard.'

'It has.'

'How come?'

I shook my head.

'I'll let you know when I find out.'

35

Animals with Men's Eyes

I couldn't stop thinking about the man who called himself Volatore and the weirdness of his visit. He wasn't *my* Volatore; who was he and *what* was he? Was the idea of Volatore like a garment to be worn by random strangers?

I was hanging on to sanity like a fallen climber clutching an unreliable tuft of grass on the face of a cliff. What about the painting? He'd said that the idea of it had come to him in a dream. What did that mean? Was the dream of tiny, tiny dancing giants waiting around for whoever might fall into it? Was the dream permanent while the dreamers came and went? Was the dream reality? And what we called reality, what was that? Our eyes give us visual data and our brains choose what pictures to make.

My mind was freewheeling through words and images. My hand went to the bookshelves and came back with

Collected Poems of Wallace Stevens. Slips of paper marking pages here and there. I opened the book to 'On an Old Horn', read:

> The bird kept saying that birds had once been men,
> Or were to be, animals with men's eyes . . .

I closed the book and watched my hand replace it on the shelf. Animals with men's eyes.

I slept badly that night. Bad dreams. A blackness that kept swooping and opening in front of me. With the smell of the man who called himself Volatore and whose feet had walked him to where I was.

Next day he did not show up. The painting stood there doing its thing as before.

'You think he's coming back?' said Olivia.

'No.'

'What about this thing with the tiny, tiny dancing whatnots? What do you think we can get for it?'

'Maybe seventy-five thousand.'

'From?'

'Mrs Goldfarb.'

'Should we phone her?'

'No. She's about due for a visit. Let her discover it for herself.'

While we and the tiny, tiny dancing giants waited I decided to see if I could track down Volatore Two. From the brown paper of the painting's wrapping there remained a bit of plastic tape. *Cosmo's Art Supply* printed on it. I knew the store because it was near the Green Apple on Clement Street in the Richmond, where I had bought my *Orlando Furioso*.

Cosmo's is one of those specialist places where the proprietor seems inseparable from his stock, as though the shelves and their contents had generated a keeper to look after them. Cosmo knows where everything is and remembers infallibly who has bought what and when. He's a tall man, jowly, bags under his eyes, hair in his ears, walks with a stoop and chain-smokes Golden Virginia roll-ups. There were a few other people examining brushes, tubes of paint and paintbox-easels and taking in the satisfying smell of a place that has what you're looking for. Cosmo ignored them and came to me.

'I need a reducing glass,' I said in order to buy something.

'Things getting too big for you?'

'It happens.'

He fetched it, I paid for it.

'Anything else?' he said.

'Do you recall a customer with a rather strong smell?' I asked him.

'Is he wanted for something?'

'Why? Did he look like a criminal to you?'

'Certainly *smelled* unlawful.'

'As far as I know, he's done nothing he could be arrested for. What did he buy?'

'Best linen canvas, stretchers, palette, palette cups,

palette knife, brushes, turps, Venice turps, stand oil, damar varnish, linseed oil, Windsor Newton cadmium yellow light, cadmium yellow deep, yellow ochre . . .'

'Outfitted himself from scratch, did he? How'd he pay? Cash, cheque, credit card?'

'Cheque: Lenore Goldfarb. Pacific National Bank, four hundred twenty-three dollars and seventy-two cents.'

'Lenore Goldfarb!'

'You know her?'

'She's one of our best customers at the Eidolon Gallery.'

Cosmo pursed his lips, blew out his breath, and made a hand gesture that signified the smallness of the world.

Mrs Goldfarb is a piece of work. By experts. She's a statuesque blonde who looks thirty-five and is two or three decades older. Her husband has a chain of shops called Bling It On. The main store is on Post Street and there are others in Los Angeles and Carmel. Lenore wears Prada but mostly she's a walking display of her husband's merchandise and the overall effect is that of a chandelier. Some women like her are into tennis and golf pros. With Mrs G it's artists, whatever kind is available.

I thanked Cosmo for his help and returned to the gallery where I found Mrs Goldfarb standing in front of the tiny, tiny etc.

'Don't try to sell me that,' she said. 'I already own it. Here's my receipt.'

I read, in her firm script: 'Received from Mrs Lenore Goldfarb $50,000 for the painting *Tiny, Tiny Dancing Giants in the Dim Red Caverns of Sleep.* (Signed) Volatore.' The signature looked crazed.

'Have you given him any money?' she said.

'No. Where is he now?'

'That's what I'd like to know. Sell the painting if you can, I bought it on impulse but it turns my stomach now. You can take your usual commission on the fifty thousand and keep anything you get over that.'

'How'd you meet him?' I asked her.

'Why do you want to know?'

'This guy is involved in my personal life somehow and I'm trying to figure it out.'

'Involved sexually?'

'No, metaphysically.'

'Well, different strokes for different folks, I guess.'

'Was it sexual with you?'

'Ladies don't tell.' Which meant that it wasn't.

'So anyhow, your first meeting with him?'

'In the Green Apple. I was looking at a two-volume paperback *Orlando Furioso* when I noticed this smell and there he was. "Ever been to El Paso?" he said.

' "No,' I said. "Why?"

'He got the Italian edition off the shelf and showed me the cover illustration. "They have this painting by Girolamo da Carpi in the museum in El Paso," he said. "Ruggiero saving Angelica from the sea monster." He was wearing a very dirty T-shirt with the short sleeves rolled up even shorter to expose his muscular arms. "Riding this guy," he said as he pointed to the da Carpi hippogriff, riderless, tattooed on his left wrist. "He's on my left because he got left, but one of these days . . ." The naked Angelica was on his right wrist. He crossed his wrists so that the hippogriff covered Angelica and leered at me.

' "Unusual," I said. "How'd you come to choose that motif?"

' "Saw it in a tattoo parlour. The tattoo artist had a print of the painting and he told me who the characters were. Right then I could feel how the hippogriff must have felt, so I told the tattooist to leave out Ruggiero when he did my hippogriff." Once I had that part of the story on me I went to the library and borrowed the two-volume paperback.

' "You're interested in art?" I said.

'He seemed to think about it for a while, then he said, "I paint a little."

' "Got anything to show me?" I said.

' "I could paint something for you," he said, "but I've got nothing to do it with."

' "Why not?" I said. "Are you on the run?"

' "Just walking around," he said. "Do you want to see what I can do or not?"

'The rest is history. Let me know when you sell the tiny, tinies.'

She glittered and tinkled out and there we were, wondering whether we'd ever find someone to take that painting off our hands. But more than that I was wondering about my Volatore: was he trying to reach me but unable to zero in on me?

36

A Sudden Kind of Thing

There's been a Mehitabel-looking cat hanging around the entrance to my building. I don't know what she does for a living. Raids the garbage cans, maybe. Only one eye – she looks as if she's knocked about a bit and *been* knocked about more than a bit. When I came home today she looked at me with a look that said, 'Well?'

'You talking to me?' I said.

'I don't see nobody else here, do you?'

'So?'

'So are you taking me in or what?'

'This is kind of sudden.'

'Life's a sudden kind of thing, baby.'

'Why me?'

'Because you know what I'm saying, OK?'

When I'd been thinking cat I'd been thinking Persian maybe or Siamese, strictly upmarket felines. Now here was this upstart vagrant from nowhere with ideas beyond her station. A hardcore optimist.

'OK, Cunégonde,' I said. 'We'll give it a try.'

'What kind of a name is that?'

'You have to read Voltaire.'

'Whatever you say, Boss.' She rubbed against my leg, purring like an outboard motor with a bad cold.

'You've got fleas, right?'

'Gimme a break, I come from a broken home.'

'What other kind is there? Wait a minute.' I found an empty Napa Valley carton and put it in front of her.

'I can take a hint,' she said, and jumped into it.

I didn't want to be seen in the elevator with my Napa Valley cast, so I carried her up the three flights to my apartment. When Cunégonde jumped out of the box I tore up Sunday's *Chronicle* into strips, filled the box with my improvised cat litter, primed it and put it in a corner of the kitchen.

'Your temporary bathroom,' I said.

She sniffed it and said, 'Roger that, Boss. Is it chow time yet?'

I spread the 'Datebook' of the paper on the floor, filled a bowl with milk, opened a can of sardines, put them in a dish, and said, 'Your table is ready, Madame. I'm going out for supplies. If the phone rings, don't answer it. Back soon.'

I went to Noe Valley Pet where I consulted with Annie and bought Frontline for the fleas, cat litter, a litter tray, a basket and blanket for my new friend's bed, and some catnip for recreational use. I had briefly considered a rubber mouse but rejected it as being an insult to a cat who had probably dined on rats or indeed anything that couldn't dine on her. I stopped off at Decamere for six cans of Whiskas, and thus laden arrived at my apartment.

'Honey, I'm home!' I called as I opened the door.

37

Every Valley

Shall be exalted? Every single one, really? KDFC got a Handel on Easter with *Messiah*, all two hours and seventeen minutes of it. In spite of my outburst on the isle of Ebuda I am not a religious person. Jewish to the core, yes, but that's my personal identity, nothing to do with God who, being omnipotent, has had the power to imagine Himself into being with all attendant perks and privileges.

He certainly convinced George Frideric Handel, who made a career out of his devotion to that exigent deity. It's hard to be sure which came first. Did God invent Handel or did Handel invent God? Not forgetting that the same arrangement existed between Him and Johann Sebastian Bach. The whole thing is confusing and I dwell on it because there is more to it than meets the mind.

'I know that my Redeemer liveth,' sings the soprano. From what are we redeemed? Original sin? Unoriginal sin? I think uncertainty is what we are redeemed from by this redeemer whom we have invested with the power to redeem us. The extra-strength placebo. If you think it works, it will.

And, unaccountably, it does. Listening to *Messiah* I feel redeemed.

38

Calamari, Hali But Not Really

'Listen, Angelica,' said Clancy when I finally stopped cutting him short on the telephone, 'I know I behaved shamefully the other day, but is that a good enough reason to break off a long-standing friendship? I apologise wholeheartedly and I promise never to turn nasty again.'

'OK, Clancy, I accept your apology and we can be friends again.'

'Will you have dinner with me this evening? No improper advances, I give you my word.'

I said yes, and we went to a restaurant in the Mission, Delfina on 18th Street. It was crowded and noisy but cheerful. Although the lighting was not intimate the many ceiling lamps were friendly. Above the voices and the clatter of cutlery I could hear the nimble arabesques of John Coltrane's saxophone in 'Like Sonny', one of the tracks I have at home.

'It's nice here,' I said to Clancy, feeling as I spoke more than a little crazed. This place was here with us in it while somewhere else was a nowhere with Volatore in it.

'And you haven't even tasted the food yet,' said Clancy.

'You order for me, OK?'

'Right, but first we need to get something sparkly down our necks.'

My attention wandered while he instructed the wine waiter who returned with a bottle and uncorked it, indicating by his expression that Clancy knew what was what. He poured a taster, and when Clancy nodded he poured the golden brightness for both of us.

'Here's looking at you,' said Clancy.

'Here's looking right back,' I replied dutifully as we touched glasses.

It was a very good dinner, with calamari followed by halibut, more sparkling wines, profiteroles, coffee and grappa. All of it delicious and all of it wasted on me. We took turns speaking but it wasn't conversation. Reality, even when supported by sensory proof, is all in the mind. And the whole evening, Clancy included, was simply not real. No wings, no air rushing past me, no world unrolling below.

When he took me home he said, 'Probably you're not going to ask me up for a nightcap.'

'I'm sorry, Clancy. It's a reality thing.'

'Yeah, right,' he snarled, and drove away.

I was glad to see him go. I was looking forward to a little Jack Daniel's, some Padre Antonio Soler with the volume down to a whisper, and a cosy chat with Cunégonde whose name no longer seemed right. This cat was more of an Irene. I'd Frontlined her fleas earlier, so she curled up in my lap and purred her satisfaction until it was time to call it a day. I put her in her basket, said, 'Goodnight, Irene,' and went to the bathroom. When I came out in my pyjamas Irene was comfortably arranged in my bed and purring so the windows rattled. A real mezzo but no seguidilla.

'Move over,' I said, and drifted off to sleep.

39

Lunarity of Volatore

Woe! Woe is me! Neither here nor gone, I wax and wane like the moon. And in the dark of the moon I wait in terror, not knowing if I shall ever reach the full again.

How did I dare to break through the boundaries of literary reality! I am a freak, a metaphysical anomaly, an existential desperado, an impossibility that slipped through the net of not-being. Angelica, let me be with you or let me die!

40

Once There Was a King

'Nothing happens on a Thursday,' said Olivia. 'Why don't we close up and go for a drive?'

'Where to?' I said.

'Ocean Beach.'

'What for?'

'I want to see the Giant Camera. I've never been to it before. Have you?'

'No, but I'm not sure a giant camera is what I need right now.'

'When in doubt, try something new,' said Olivia. So we shut up shop and off we went.

Olivia's car is a 1941 Lincoln Continental, white. It's a classic and she claims it pulls a more intellectual type than the Porsche she used to drive. The car's name is Lucille.

'It's what B.B. King calls his guitar,' she told me. 'Seemed right for this baby.'

'Lucille is in a country song too,' I said. About leaving her husband with hungry children and a crop still to harvest.'

'Takes all kinds of Lucilles,' said Olivia. 'Same as it takes all kinds of Angelicas. And dads.'

'Aha! I noticed him scoping your legs.'

'He's going to do a portrait of me.'

'Are you sure it's your face he's interested in?'

'Jesus, Ange, what is it with you today? Why do you have to rain on my parade?'

'Sorry, Liv. I'm a little down today and I guess I don't want anybody else to be too up. But can I say something about your upcoming portrait session?'

'Feel free.'

'He'll probably do preliminary sketches and most likely he'll ask for quick poses, fifteen minutes or less.'

'So?'

'To get to the essential you he'll want you to take your clothes off.'

'Isn't that what they all want?'

'I just thought you should be prepared.'

'I'm always prepared, Ange. Do you have some kind of problem with this?'

'Right. Sorry, I'll back off.'

We were driving through the Richmond. The sea was on our left, apartment blocks on our right. There's just one kind of urban coastal sunlight, whether it's in San Francisco or Atlantic City or Civitavecchia. It's flat,

146

it's hard, there's no give to it. Colours recede into glare. Trees look stupefied. Buildings and road signs and billboards spring up like toadstools in the darkness of that light.

'Have we stopped talking now?' said Olivia.

'No, I just don't have anything to say at the moment.'

'Can I ask you something?'

'Go ahead.'

'That weird guy with the smell who called himself Volatore, he really got to you, didn't he?'

'Yes, he did.'

'Him and that painting that almost made us fall over, and that business with *Orlando Furioso* – the things he knew. He said he must have read it but he didn't strike me as that much of a reader. You said you were going to tell me why that whole thing hit you so hard when you found out yourself.'

'OK, Liv. If I told you I've had sex with an imaginary animal, what would your reaction be?'

'An *imaginary* animal?'

'That's right.'

'What kind of imaginary animal?'

'A hippogriff.'

'*A hippogriff!*'

'Named Volatore.'

'*Volatore!*'

'Does repeating everything in italics help you to take it in?'

'Yes. I'm trying to get my head around this imaginary business. Like, did you name your vibrator Volatore and build a whole fantasy around it?'

'I haven't got a vibrator. And I didn't build a fantasy. He appeared at my window one evening. Emma Kirkby singing "Olimpia's Lament" lifted him up to my apartment. Solid and real, in 3-D with a funky animal smell. One thing led to another and we had sex.'

'Wasn't he too big for you?'

'He thought himself smaller.'

'Ange, what kind of a relationship did you have with your father when you were growing up?'

'Why do you ask?'

'Might this Volatore be an imaginative displacement of sexual longings for your father?'

'Jesus! Do they print that on the backs of cornflakes boxes now?'

'Come on, Ange I'm only trying to help.'

'Let's leave shrinkable matters to our respective shrinks, OK? Can we talk about something else? Or maybe we could have a little music?'

Olivia had installed an up-to-the-minute radio and CD player in Lucille and there was a small rack of CDs fitted to the dashboard: Julian Bream; Peggy Lee; Teresa Berganza in *Carmen*, Alfred Deller singing Henry Purcell; Rossini's *La cenerentola*, an opera not in my father's collection nor my own. This was a 1994 recording with the orchestra and chorus of the Royal Opera

House of Covent Garden, London, Jennifer Larmore as Cinderella.

'What's in the player now?' I asked Olivia.

'Act I of the one you're looking at,' she said. 'My uncle Leon died and left me his collection. I was just starting to listen to it when I picked you up. It's on track 3 now.'

I took the booklet out of the box and found track 3:

CENERENTOLA
(con fono flemmatico}
Una voltac'era un re
che a star solo annoio . . .

CINDERELLA
(singing to herself)
Once there was a king
who was bored with being all alone . . .

'Oh!' I said. Because those words all at once seemed to be talking to me. I pushed the start button and the voice of the poor daughter, motherless and discarded by her father, humble among the ashes, came to me pensive and slow. The song, with its little story of a lonely king who searched and searched until he found the pure and innocent girl he wanted – why did it make me cry? To me it was a *Volatore* song of heartbreak and hopeful longing, the essence of it not the comedic lightness that Rossini was famous for but something deep and sad that slipped past him. Was Volatore my lonely king? Of course I may be knitting with one needle, that certainly can't be ruled out. Olivia tactfully made no comment and kept her eyes on the road.

At Ocean Beach we climbed the hill to Cliff House. Next to the bar there were stairs that went around back and there was the Giant Camera, a structure looking like a huge 35-mm camera lying on its back with its lens pointing at the sky.

'It's a camera obscura,' said Olivia. 'Leonardo da Vinci invented it. Vermeer and Canaletto used little ones, just a box with a lens in front and a ground-glass screen at the back.'

We waited with other obscurophiles and paid three dollars each as we came out of the sunlight into the camera body. We went through a door and into the dark chamber; before us on the round viewing table was a brilliant circle of brightness in which there were seals basking on a large rock by the dazzling blue Pacific. The camera operator told us what we were seeing as he rotated the lens to the marine headland and back to Cliff House.

We came blinking out into the sunlight.

'OK, Olivia,' I said, 'we went into a dark chamber and saw the world around us very bright. Is that it?'

'The clarity of the view was terrific!' she insisted. 'Maybe you have to go into a dark chamber to see the world clearly.'

I didn't say anything. I had found the contrast between the darkness and the brightness aggravating, like the tongue going into the cavity of an aching tooth. Unreasonable of me but then I'm not an altogether reasonable person.

'Now that we've had the metaphor,' I said, 'maybe we could get some lunch?'

We went to Sutro's at the Cliff House where we had beer-braised black mussels with frites and Veuve Clicquot which made the world a little easier to take.

As we drove back to town the sky was not yet dark but the street lights were on and the lights in the houses. That time of day always brings an ache to my throat. I feel that all those, now gone, who have known this gentle goodbye from the day that is passing, never to return, are seeing it through my eyes. Volatore also seeing it through my eyes. '"Look thy last on all things lovely, every hour . . ."' I sang under my breath, like Cinderella crouching in the ashes.

Olivia notices everything.

'I think you need to pull yourself together, Angie,' she said. 'Maybe you just need to get laid. Didn't you have something going with Clancy?'

'Been there, done that,' I said. 'It didn't work for me.'

'OK, maybe Clancy didn't float your boat. But this Volatore shit is going to drive you crazy if you don't let go of it.'

'You're right, Liv – I'll try to do better.'

When she dropped me off I stepped wearily into the bleakness of the street lamps, the shadows and the mica sparkles on the pavement. In the past, easing through those lamps and shadows and sparkles, I used to wish I had a cat waiting for me. Now Irene was waiting. She'd rub against my leg and purr, then she'd keep me company and dab at the foam while I had a hot bath. There'd be a large Jack Daniel's beside the tub, and on the Bose, warm and golden and shadowy, the strings of Monsieur de Sainte-Colombe.

41

Passing, Never to Return

'Passing, never to return!' These words have come into my mind like some melancholy refrain that refuses to go away. Passing, passing, never to return! What? Everything? Angelica and Volatore both? Shall we cease to be imagined? Shall we pass like the fading of the day, like breath upon a mirror, suddenly gone?

42

Mostly Like a Horse

He calls himself Volatore and he is not *my* Volatore. But he smells like him. An olfactory mystery. I went to the Mission Police Station on Valencia and 17th. Once there I stood looking at the *Seven Dancing Stars* for a while. I don't like to miss meaningful signs of any kind, and these boulders set in the floor, representing the Pleiades, might well have some significance for me. These seven sisters of mythology, daughters of Atlas, are named in *Lemprière's Classical Dictionary* as Alcyone, Merope, Maia, Electra, Taygeta, Sterope and Celeno. Merope's star is dim because she married a mortal. A warning about mixed marriages? The constellation is near the back of Taurus in the zodiac.

There was a sort of bank teller's window in the wall behind the elevator.

'I want to report a missing person,' I said.

This got me to a Sergeant Hennessy, a large bear of a man whose look and manner made me want to climb into his lap and tell him everything that was troubling me. I think he sensed this because he remained standing at a safe distance.

'OK,' he said after I had identified myself. 'Who's missing?'

'A man who calls himself Volatore.'

'Sounds like an opera. Is that his first name or his last name?'

'He says it's his only name.'

'Relation of yours?'

'No.'

'Friend?'

'Sort of.'

'Where and when did you last see him?'

'At the Eidolon Gallery in the Mission four or five days ago. I'm not sure – it's been a confusing time for me.'

'Describe him.'

'Over six feet tall, strongly built; long black hair, long face, high cheekbones, blue eyes. Wearing black jeans, blue denim shirt, Timberland boots, all new. Paint smears on everything.'

'Any identifying marks?'

'A naked-woman tattoo on his right wrist and a hippogriff on his left wrist.'

'You don't have to explain what a hippogriff is – I read sci-fi fantasy.'

'Plus he's got a smell.'

'What kind of smell?'

I almost said. 'A hippogriff smell,' but I caught myself in time and said, 'Mostly like a horse.'

'*Mostly* like a horse. Anything else in his smell?'

'Some other kind of animal I didn't recognise. But you can't mistake the smell.'

'Right: mostly like a horse. That narrows it down. OK, we'll give you a call when we have anything to report.'

At home I got my big *Maps of the Heavens* off the shelf and turned to Albrecht Dürer's 'Northern Hemisphere'. I searched for Taurus but couldn't find him, let alone the Pleiades. No luck with anyone else's 'Northern Hemisphere' either. 'OK,' I said. I went to my PC and googled for Seven Sisters Road, figuring there probably was one somewhere in San Francisco. This took me by devious routes to some beautiful Victorian houses in Alamo Square. At that point my search frenzy left me and I went to the gallery where I spent the rest of the day cataloguing Alyosha Zhabotinsky.

I expected a long wait for any result and I had misgivings about the possible waste of police time but the next day I had a call from Sergeant Hennessy.

'We've got a man here who answers your description except no smell, wrong name and fifty thousand dollars. Would you know anything about that?'

'Yes, I would. He didn't steal it.'

'He says his name is Joe Fontana and he doesn't know you. If you'd like to have a look at him come to the station today because we've got nothing but a vagrancy charge to hold him on. Unless you've got some other charge to make.'

'Where'd you find him?' I said.

'He was sleeping on a veranda in Alamo Square. The owners of the house were away but a neighbour reported a vagrant on the premises.'

'You guys sure work fast. I'll be right over.'

When I arrived at the station Sergeant Hennessy showed me into what I suppose was a small interrogation room where the artist formerly known as Volatore was sitting at a table.

'Is this going to be distressing for you in any way?' Hennessy asked me.

'No,' I said, 'it isn't that kind of thing.'

'Right,' he said. 'Here's Mr Fontana. No ID, no address, new clothes and Timberlands with paint smears. And fifty thousand smackers.'

'That's him,' I said.

'Shall I leave you to it,' said Hennessy, 'or do you want me to stick around?'

'Please do – I'm sure you're better at asking useful questions than I am.'

'You start and I'll stand by for the time being.' To Fontana he said, 'I've already told you that you're not charged with anything but vagrancy. This lady thinks you might be able to help her.'

'OK,' said Fontana to me. 'How can I help you?'

'Why did you tell me your name was Volatore?'

'I've never heard that name till now and I've never seen you before.'

'Do you remember where you got the fifty thousand dollars?'

'I didn't even know I had it until the cops frisked me and counted it.'

'You don't remember doing a painting?'

'You mean a picture?'

'Yes.'

'No, I wouldn't know about anything like that.'

'Forgive me if my questions seem strange. Can you recall any weird dreams you've had lately?'

'Dreams are personal.'

'Of course they are.'

'So why should I tell you mine? I've got fifty thousand bucks that I didn't steal and I can stop being a vagrant and answering questions.'

'Calm down,' said Hennessy. 'Maybe I'll book you for committing public nuisance.'

'What public nuisance?'

'Peeing in the bushes in Alamo Square. Now answer the lady.'

'Dreams?' I said.

'No.' To Hennessy he said, 'Go ahead and book me for peeing in the bushes, I'm pretty sure I can pay the fine. Whatever dreams I have belong to me and nobody else.'

'Do you remember Lenore Goldfarb?' I asked him.

'No. Should I?'

'She paid you that money for a painting.'

'I never heard of the lady.'

'I can arrange for her to refresh your memory.'

'What for?'

'She paid you that money for a painting that came from a dream. The painting is in the Eidolon Gallery now. Would you like to see it?'

'No.'

'This is kind of interesting,' said Hennessy. 'Do you want us to take him to your gallery?'

'Yes, please.'

'I don't think I have to agree to that,' said Fontana.

'Yes, you do,' said Hennessy, 'or I may have to take you in hand for resisting arrest.'

'But I haven't resisted arrest.'

'That can be arranged, fella.'

So we went to the gallery and Hennessy stood Fontana in front of the painting.

'Funny thing,' said Hennessy, 'looking at that makes me a little woozy.'

'What about *him*?' said Olivia.

Fontana was lying on the floor. He had fainted. We brought him around with a little cold water in his face and sat him up. The paintings on the walls suddenly looked empty, as if the virtue had left them. Paintings! I thought, what an odd thing to do.

'Can I go now?' said Fontana.

'What about the painting?' I asked him. 'It's your own work.'

'I don't remember doing it and looking at it makes me a little sick. I don't know what else I can tell you.'

By this time I was pretty sure that Hennessy felt as Olivia and I did: Fontana was the victim of some kind of temporary mind alteration and was still in a frail state.

'Where are you going when you leave here?' Hennessy asked him.

'First I'll get myself a place, then I'll think what to do next.'

'Here's my card,' said Hennessy. 'Phone me and tell me where you'll be. I don't want you to pass out somewhere and be lying unfound for days.'

'Thanks,' said Fontana.

'Give you a lift anywhere?' said Hennessy.

'That's a lot of money to be carrying around,' I said. 'We can keep most of it here in the safe for you or open an account for you at our bank.'

'OK,' said Fontana. He had fifty thousand-dollar bills. He peeled off one and gave me the rest. 'Please just keep it here for now,' he said.

'So?' said Hennessy. 'Lift?'

'Thanks,' said Fontana. 'I'm going to do some walking to clear my head.'

With that he left. Odourlessly, the man who was not my Volatore.

43

Farnesses of Tinyness

I am confused, forlorn, full of doubts. Again and again I try to send my thoughts and fears to Angelica but there is no response from her. Have my messages gone astray? Is she sending messages to me?

Now I wonder how things have come to this pass. How did I come to be stranded in this nowhereness, half out of one reality, half into another? Where and when was the beginning of it? My memory is scattering into dancing colours, blurs and flashes swooping to escarpments of eyes, caverns of listening, farnesses of tinyness. A sorcerer told me to go where I went, I looked into an eye and saw the beginning or was it the end of me?

44

Dos Arbolitos, *Endlessly Rocking*

I gave Dr Levy notice and moved on to my third shrink, Dr Long. Dave Michnik, one of our painters, said he was a no-bullshit guy. Dr Long worked out of a houseboat called *Dos Arbolitos* at Sausalito. The dancing ripple pattern on the ceiling was reassuring and the gentle lapping of the water endlessly rocking made me feel sleepy and safe.

'*Dos Arbolitos*,' I said. 'Two little trees.'

'You know the song?'

'I've got a CD with it but all I remember is the title and the fact that it's a *huapango*. Is there a story behind that name for your houseboat?'

'There's a story behind everything but let's talk about you.'

Dr Long was a tall man in jeans and a denim shirt. He had startling blue eyes and a long face that always seemed ready to – and frequently did – break into a half-smile.

'You don't look like a shrink,' I said.

'I charge like one though,' he said. 'What can I do for you? If anything.'

'I have a reality problem.'

'That's called life.'

'But I'm living in two realities. Maybe more.'

'And?'

'I'm trying to understand them, trying to define what they are.'

'Why?'

'So I'll know, so I can deal with them.'

'Knowing won't help. That's a waste of energy. Get practical.'

'How?'

'It doesn't matter how many realities there are or what they are; just handle them one at a time and do whatever needs to be done.'

'That's theory; practice is something else. I want to talk about Volatore Two.'

'But you haven't told me about Volatore One yet.'

So I told him all there was to tell about Volatore.

'And I still don't know if it was real. I mean, how can a woman have sex with an imaginary creature that only exists in a book?'

'*Everything* is real – try to remember that.'

'Even a hallucination?'

'Even a hallucination. You experienced it; whatever it was, it happened to you and is part of your reality.'

163

'You're batting a thousand, Doc. I'm ready to throw away my placebos. Have you read *Orlando Furioso*, by the way?'

'Yes, I have. Did you make up the name Volatore?'

'No, he, the hippogriff, told it to me.'

'Are you in love with him?'

'Yes, but I want him to be somebody I can walk down the street with, and he can only assume human form if he takes over someone else's body. I've told you all that.'

'What if you *did* walk down the street with him in his original hippogriff form – do you think other people would see him?'

'I'm afraid to try that experiment. Can we move on to Volatore Two?'

'OK.'

'He had the same smell and he knew about the painting of Ruggiero and Angelica in El Paso. He himself did a weird painting while in a sort of trance, then he came out of it, didn't remember doing the painting, and hasn't painted since. I keep wondering if Volatore played any part in that.'

'Where is the original Volatore now?'

'I don't know. Somehow we dropped out of the Ariosto story and now we've lost touch.'

'Have you tried to contact him?'

'No, this double-reality stress got to be too much for me and I've just been trying to get my head straight for a while now.'

'Do you *want* to find him?'

'Yes, I do.'

'So will you try to reach him now?'

'Yes, I will. It's something I have to think about.'

'What is there to think about?'

'How to do it.'

'Don't you know how?' The ripple pattern on the ceiling was moving faster, as if speeded up by his voice.

'It's a trial-and-error thing,' I said, 'and I'll have to do it in my own time if you'll allow me.'

'You sound defensive.'

'Yes.'

'Why?'

'I feel attacked.'

'I'm not attacking you.'

I looked at my watch.

'Isn't my time up?' I said. 'You probably have some-one coming for your next session.'

Dr Long shook his head.

'Is it possible,' he said, 'that you're not altogether sure you *want* to be with Volatore again?'

'I have to go now,' I said. 'I'm expected elsewhere.'

45

Random Passes, Wide Receivers

Olivia Partridge, my partner at Eidolon, is more of a pragmatist than I am; her thinking always leads to action.

'We promised Ossip Przewalski a new show,' she said, 'a while before our recent Volatore binge, remember?'

'I remember.'

'So let's do it, OK?'

'OK.'

Przewalski rides a Harley Davidson and he paints nudes on Harley Davidsons. His approach is somewhere between Kokoschka and Redon and his last show was a sell-out. We swung into action planning the layout of the show, composing the ad for the art magazines, making up the invitation list and organising the catering.

I did this automatically while my mind was on other things. Sometimes I ask myself whether being human in the usual way is enough. Whether something isn't missing. Some animality in another dimension. Well, I would say that, wouldn't I? I have coupled with an imaginary beast and I can still see his strange eyes, his beaked face close to mine. Not a dream, not a hallucination. Part of my humanity. Maybe I'm not the only one. Maybe others have had imaginary-animal lovers.

Dr Long says not to bother with definitions but to deal with things in the simplest way practical. Occam's razor and all that. But what *is* the simplest way? It seems that the original Volatore is transmitting something of himself to receivers who don't necessarily have any connection with him. Joe Fontana had read *Orlando Furioso* and knew about the da Carpi painting but Alyosha Zhabotinsky, who might have read Gogol but not Ariosto was picking up scrambled Volatorisms such as 'dim red taverns of sheep'. Are these the people he's trying to reach? Not likely. He's firing off random shots because he's unable to aim his transmissions. I know he's trying to reach *me*.

Dr Long asked me whether I was sure I wanted to be with Volatore again. *Am* I sure? Well, no. It's a heavy trip, and scary because I sense in it the danger of losing my mind. R. D. Laing said, at the height of his vogue in the seventies, that the breakdown is often the breakthrough but that idea hasn't had too many adherents lately and I don't think it would work for me. I'm afraid of falling through a hole in reality if I keep messing with two kinds of it. So are my fears and doubts creating a barrier to communication from Volatore? I won't think about that any more right now, I'll think about other things.

46

Expectation

'Irene,' I said. 'You're losing your figure.'

'But you're gaining a litter,' said the look she gave me.

'So who's the father?'

'I didn't see his face – it was a speed-dating kind of thing.'

'Maybe it's time to have you spayed.'

'What, you don't believe in free love?'

'Irene, nothing about love is free.'

'Has life made you bitter? Talk to me about it, I'm a good listener.'

'Some other time, Irene. Now I have to think of names for your love-children.'

'You're all heart, Boss.'

47

Cometh the Hour

The painting stayed on the easel. We hadn't framed it and we mostly kept it covered. People came and went; for some, but not many, we uncovered it but it stayed unsold. One day the Volatore smell walked in, bearing on its waves a small man with a beautiful hairpiece that concealed his baldness so realistically that it was like the acting of a method actor whose realism emphasises the artfulness of his art. This man was wearing Armani, Rolex and a confident smile. He had a red–carpet kind of walk; in his small way he was grandiose.

Olivia and I uncovered the tiny, tinies and stood on either side of his avenue of approach. He looked at the painting, sighed, closed his eyes, opened them and turned to us, at the same time taking out a large chequebook.

'How much?' he said.

It was a moment or two before I was able to take in the reality of his words.

'You want to buy it?' I said.

He nodded, and speaking slowly, as to a foreigner, said, 'It is for this reason that I flourish my large chequebook.'

'This one speaks to you, does it?' said Olivia.

He closed his eyes again.

'In a dream have I been there with the tiny, tiny dancing giants in the dim red caverns of sleep.'

'Have you had this dream recently?' I asked him.

'Yes. Why do you ask?'

'This is the first time I've heard of anyone seeing the subject of a painting in a dream before seeing the actual painting. You don't happen to know Lenore Goldfarb, do you?'

'This pleasure,' he said, 'I have not yet had. Again I flourish my chequebook and express my wish to know the price of this painting.'

'This one is a rarity,' I said. 'In fact it's unique, the only work of a man who gave up painting after producing it.'

'As one would,' said the odoriferous gentleman, uncapping his Mont Blanc. 'I am ready if you are.'

'Very well then.' I drew a deep breath. 'The price is one hundred and fifty thousand dollars.'

Unperturbed, he found a table to lean on, wrote the cheque in a large round hand, waved it in the air once or twice to dry the ink, and presented it to me. I looked at the signature: 'Volatore'.

'Volatore!' I exclaimed.

'Ah,' he said preenfully, 'this name makes a bell to ring, yes?'

'Yes. Tell me why.'

'Do you go to the movies?'

'Sometimes. Are you an actor?'

'Actors! Pfft!' (With a snap of the fingers.) Have you seen *A Midnight too Far*?'

'I've seen it,' said Olivia. 'Lola Trotter and Rodney Stark.'

'And the credits?' said Volatore. 'Did you read the credits?'

'No.'

He passed his hand over his wig and gave us a sidelong glance.

'Hairstylist!' said Olivia.

'Hairstylist!' he said, drawing himself up to his full shortness. 'I, Volatore, made of Miss Trotter a thing of beauty, Ah! *che bellezza*! Without my art she would receive from no one a second glance.'

'You've done a great job on her,' said Olivia.

'Thank you,' said Volatore, bowing modestly. 'I am also known for Volatore's TurboScalp System (patent pending) which has stimulated Mr Stark's performance to a level well beyond the limits of his talent.'

'Can a TurboScalp System really do that?'

'He thinks it does, so it does. This is known as the placebo effect.'

'Interesting!'

'Yes, and profitable as well. High-powered executives, athletes, opera singers and many other professionals who must work to the highest standards swear by my TurboScalp System. It is because of this that my cheque-book is so virile.'

'Forgive me if I'm being too personal,' I said, 'but your smell . . .'

'Ah, the smell of me!'

'Yes, as you have to get close to your clients, doesn't it present a problem?'

'No. Only when I am receiving a transmission does the smell manifest itself. In my salon it happens not.'

'So you're receiving a transmission now?'

'As your nose tells you.'

'From whom?' said Olivia.

Volatore shrugged and with both hands made a 'It's a mystery to me' gesture.

'It's a mystery to me,' he said.

'If you don't mind my asking,' I said, 'is your name always Volatore?'

'What do you mean?'

'I mean, is it Volatore every day or only on special days?'

'My name is what you call a twenty-four-seven thing, every day of the year.'

'Please don't be offended by these personal questions,' I I said, 'but has it always been Volatore?'

'Ah,' he said. 'Only since 1958. In that year there was a popular song that was a big hit: "*Nel blu dipinto di blu*" was the title but it became known as "Volare" which is the infinitive "to fly".' He sang a few bars of the song. 'My father liked the sound of that word, and he went on to the word for "flyer" which he liked even better, and he had the family name legally changed from Garzanti to Volatore.'

'Tell me,' I said, 'what do you think is the special attribute that made you a receiver of these mysterious transmissions?'

'This to me is also a mystery,' said the hairstylist with the appropriate gesture.

'Do you know why Orlando is furious?' asked Olivia whose knowledge of Ariosto was limited to the title.

'This I think must be known to everyone,' said Volatore Three. 'It began when he and Angelica drank from the two fountains, he from the one that made him love her and she from the one that made her despise him.'

'This is not common knowledge,' I said. 'Have you a particular interest in Ariosto?'

Volatore Three smiled deprecatingly.

'It is my hobby to render his Italian into English,' he said humbly. 'Mine may not be as good as what is already published but it gives me pleasure and harms no one. Ariosto's elegance and wit can be approached in more than one way in a rhyming translation.'

'Ah!' said Olivia and I together.

'Please telephone me when my cheque has cleared,' he said, 'and I shall have the painting picked up.' He handed

me his card which bore a Nob Hill address, bowed cere-
moniously, and left.

'Curiouser and curiouser,' said Olivia. 'I wonder who
Volatore Four will be.'

'Me too,' I said, and the two of us took the cheque to
the bank.

48

Cold Water

Dr Jim Long was born in Pennsylvania, and sometimes when his mind is pedalling in busy circles he recalls a thing from his youth. He recalls a drink of water from a mountain spring in the Appalachians. He was hot and sweaty and tired when he came upon a stone trough with water flowing into it from an iron pipe. Cold sparkling mountain water filling the trough from an iron pipe that was beaded with droplets of condensation. There were leaves and sand and tiny crayfish in the bottom of the trough. He plunged his face into the water and drank the best drink he would ever have in his life. The leaves of the trees were stirring in the summer breeze. Everything was more than itself.

Dos Arbolitos is both home and office for Jim, with books everywhere and various prints and posters, among them John William Waterhouse's *Naiad*. He smiles approvingly, then moves on to Waterhouse's *Destiny*, where he shakes his head in admiration. 'Yes!' he says quietly, because in those two paintings he's looking at the face and form of Angelica Greenberg. Her beauty is Victorian and she is quite simply the definitive Waterhouse woman from top to bottom. Her figure is long and lithe, her limbs all sweetly rounded, her body ideal for such naiad activities as swimming and dodging around trees. As to her face, the nose is long and elegantly retroussé; the delicately modelled cheeks echo her other roundnesses and offer to the viewer her large and lustrous sea-green eyes with their shapely brows under that shining coppery hair. Her lips are made for kissing, and her firmly rounded chin completes the face that is poised on the long and graceful neck of Angelica Waterhouse Greenberg.

'That whole first session with Angelica,' says Dr Jim to himself, 'I was showing off. The things I said were OK but when I play the session back in my head I can hear myself showing off. "It's called life,"' he says, mimicking his show-off voice. 'OK, she's a Waterhouse beauty but she's also someone who came to me for help with her problems and I'm her forty-one-year-old shrink who started with her like a sixteen-year-old high-school kid and have since abandoned all professionalism and indulge in sexual fantasies. Very good, Dr Jim. Felicity said when she moved out that I lived too much in my head and acted too much out of it. She'd have made a pretty good shrink.'

49

Death in the Afternoon

I hadn't heard from Clancy since the evening of our dinner non-event and I felt a little guilty about not being kinder to him on that occasion, so when the preparations for the Przewalski show were well in hand I went round to Clancy's Bar one afternoon. The place was crowded as usual and Himself was visible sitting at a table with a striking blonde who'd had some work done. She didn't have a sign around her neck that said *I'M SLEEPING WITH HIM* but she might as well have. They were leaning towards each other in a sleeping-together kind of way while he lit her cigarette and she lit his fire. She had very thin arms.

I was hoping to disappear unnoticed but of course he saw me.

'Hi, Angelica,' he said with the front of his voice. 'Come and join us.' So I did. 'The world doesn't stand still,' his face said to me very plainly.

'Go for it, Clance,' my face answered.

He interrupted our wordless conversation to introduce Blondie.

'Angelica, this is Nikki. Nikki, Angelica.' We shook hands. 'Angelica is one of my oldest friends,' he said smoothly.

'Carries her years well,' said Nikki.

'And without surgical assistance,' I replied.

'Nikki's published a monograph on Tanagra figurines,' boasted Clancy.

Nikki was looking into the distance, humming the seguidilla from Act I of *Carmen* softly to herself. She was the right age for Dad's ex-mid-life crisis, thirty-five or so, only five years older than I. Sitting there in her little cotton print with her thin arms and her worked-on face. The history-of-art lecturer who'd taken her to Rome, had he gone back to his wife?

'Who was the publisher?' I asked her.

'University of California Press. Are you interested in Tanagra?'

'My father had a couple of books on it. He said that although the pieces were small they had a bigness about them because of the wholeness of the artists' vision. They reminded him of Daumier in the way the gesture contained the figure.'

'What's your last name?' she asked me.

'Greenberg.'

She nodded several times, made a 'Whaddaya gonna do?' gesture, and reached for a fresh cigarette.

'Angelica,' said Clancy. 'What're you drinking?'

'Jack Daniel's, please, a small one.'

'Rocks? Water?'

'No, just as it comes from the bottle.'

When Javier brought my drink I raised my glass to Nikki and Clancy.

'Here's luck,' I said, downed it and left.

50

Trained Perfection

On the way home in the cable car I watched the motorman working the grip lever and brakes. Another metaphor: how do I grip my destiny cable? And what about the brakes? I could feel the movement of that cable under me but I didn't know how to make my life-car do anything useful.

That evening I didn't feel like going out for dinner and I didn't feel like cooking so I ordered Chinese from the Kwan-Yin. I had most of a bottle of Cava with it, scanned the TV schedule and decided to watch Rita Hayworth and Orson Welles in *The Lady from Shanghai*. Welles has never been venerated by me as much as he is generally thought to deserve but Rita Hayworth had married him and now they were both dead and she had outlived her beauty and her wits and was all gone, like champagne spilt on desert sands while her dancing flickered on demand for anyone with the necessary equipment.

Fred Astaire said that she had been his favourite partner. 'She danced with trained perfection and individuality,' were his words. 'Trained perfection'! From childhood up trained to delight an audience with the dazzle of her beauty, the grace and vividness of her movement, the spell of her charm, and to die knowing somewhere in herself that all of it was gone and she was alone except for her faithful daughter.

My mind drifted in and out of the twists of the plot, Welles's dreadful brogue, the horrible voice of the actor who played George Grisby and the passionate whispers of Rita Hayworth. Part of the film was set in San Francisco, and Welles obviously liked the noirish melancholy of the horns on the Golden Gate Bridge because he kept them blowing even when there was no fog.

The picture wound up rather like the last act of *Hamlet*: Rita Hayworth died along with the evil husband and his evil partner, and she herself was revealed as no better than she should have been. Welles and his dreadful brogue survived the whole mess – after all, he directed. The film left me unmoved but internally I was weeping for Rita Hayworth of the Dancing Cansinos who grew up to become Fred Astaire's favourite partner. I ejected the Welles film from my mind and inserted the scene from *You'll Never Get Rich* in which she and Astaire are practising a dance routine from a show they're working on. She was wearing rehearsal shorts that allowed her leg action to be fully seen. The *gallantry* of that trained perfection!

It made the world seem a better place. Not content with my mental playback, I put the DVD of the film in the player and watched it tearfully. To give so much and end with so little! I poured myself a large Laphroaig and raised my glass. 'Thank you, Rita Cansino,' I said, 'for making the world a better place while you were in it.' Then I drank it down and woke up the next morning with a bad taste in my mouth but no regrets.

51

Faintness of Volatore

Dimness and silence. Everything is moving away from me. The world and Angelica, where have they gone? I am losing the idea of me, whatever it was. Smaller and smaller I grow. I am disappearing into the nothingness of things forgotten. My name, what is it? There was one who would remember me; where is she? *Who* is she?

52

All at Sea

'Well,' said Dr Long, 'in our last session it emerged that you weren't sure you wanted to be with Volatore again.'

'I'm not sure of anything right now,' I confessed. 'I may be a figment of my own imagination.'

'But that's all anyone is; it's the human condition. We're given a name at birth and photographs are taken. We come to be known by name and face and from this we piece together an identity and fix it in memory. This identity is not physically part of us; a knock on the head can make it go away.'

'I think mine might go away without the knock on the head. Some nights I'm afraid to go to sleep for fear that I'll disappear altogether.'

'You won't though. Who are you in your dreams?'

'Me, Angelica Greenberg.'

'There, you see?'

'I know that what you're saying is meant to reassure me but it doesn't.'

'It really doesn't?'

'Yes, it really doesn't.'

'Perhaps I should take up another line of work.'

'What else can you do?'

'Maybe I'll run away to sea.'

'Doc, you're being frivolous on my time.'

'Actually, what you need is a frivolous day and a change of air. A little sea voyage on the bay might be just the thing.'

'In what? Have you got a boat other than *Dos Arbolitos*?'

'I do, and I provisioned it this morning.'

'What kind of boat is it?'

'A yawl. It's a replica of Joshua Slocum's *Spray* in which he was the first man to sail alone around the world.'

'Have you sailed alone around the world?'

'Only the world in my head.'

'What's your boat called?'

'*Mariposa*.'

'Butterfly.' I sang two lines of Dolly Parton's song about the butterfly character of love.

'This butterfly,' said Dr Long, 'is from way back. There was a Chinese philosopher called Chuang Tzu. While pondering the meaning of life he dozed off under a tree and dreamt that he was a butterfly. It was a beautiful dream and the flying was a special delight. When he woke up he said to a friend, "I am puzzled." And he told his dream.

'"So what's puzzling?" said the friend. "You had a nice dream and that's that."

'"But it was so real," said Chuang Tzu, "just as real as this conversation we're having. I thought I was Chuang Tzu dreaming of being a butterfly. But what if, at this very moment, I am a butterfly dreaming of being Chuang Tzu?"'

Here Dr Long paused and looked at me expectantly.

'Does it matter which he was?' I said.

'Very good, Angelica. You think the same as Chuang Tzu. He said that all things are united by the life force within them, that *all are one*.'

'There you go,' I said. 'Great minds.'

We got into Dr Long's old Citroën 2CV and it rattled into life.

'Please call me Jim now that we're out of the office,' he said.

'OK, Jim. Where are we going?'

'Schoonmaker Point Marina.'

'Now that we're outdoors, can I ask you some personal questions?'

'Shoot.'

'How old are you?'

'Forty-one.'

'Married?'

'Was.'

'She was one of the *dos arbolitos*?'

He nodded.

'We're divorced now. She left me for a happiness guru.'

'Then she couldn't have been right for you in the first place.'

'Now you tell me.'

'Children?'

'No.'

'Thank you. It's always a comfort to know what's what.'

'Good, I want you to be comfortable. I think I already know most of the personal facts about you.'

'All the pertinent ones, I don't think ephemera need to come into it.'

'What kind of ephemera?'

'The kind that don't last as long as it takes to tell about them.'

'Then don't tell about them – I don't want anything to interfere with this outing.'

'I won't let anything do that, Jim, I like being out with you; you're a comfortable man to be with.'

'Thank you, all encouragement gratefully received. In my office I'm reasonably confident, but out of doors with a beautiful woman I revert to my default position which is pretty shaky.'

'I don't believe a word of that but thank you for the handsome compliment.' We had turned into a parking area and I saw a lot of water and a lot of boats. The salt breeze was full of promise. 'Are we there?'

'Yup, this is Schoonmaker Point.' After parking the car he took an insulated bag out of the boot. 'I thought we might have a picnic,' he said. 'Do you like burritos?'

'Love 'em.'

'*Carne asada* and Jerry's burritos from Balazo?'

'My favourites.'

'That's the food. The drink is on board.'

'*Mariposa* has a fridge?'

'Yes. Can you guess what's in it?'

'Bollinger?'

'Right! How did you do that?'

'I thought, if I were Jim and wanted to give Angelica a really great picnic, I'd get Bollinger and burritos for the occasion.'

'What a mind! Beautiful! And the rest of you's not bad either.'

'You're very kind. But we'd better go aboard before your compliments go to my head.'

'And what happens then?'

'Who knows? I'm a creature of impulse.'

'Is that a promise?'

'Every day is a winding road, Jim.'

'Then let's not delay. *Mariposa*'s berthed over there, past the beach.'

There she was. When you get up close to any boat, even a rowing boat, you see that it's a serious thing, the self of it bigger than the size of it. Because the sea is a serious thing and all water leads to it. *Mariposa* was thirty-six feet long, a proper seagoing vessel whose original had sailed around the world in all weathers. 'Let's do it,' she whispered brazenly. 'Let's just do it.'

'She's very forthright,' I said to Jim as we stepped aboard.

'Only way to be,' he said, and pointed out the main-mast, mizzenmast, and the halyards for mainsail, jib and spanker as well as those for main gaff. Also the topping lifts. Under his guidance we hoisted sail and eased out of the dock trailing the dinghy. The prevailing wind in the bay is from the west, and *Mariposa* heeled to it a little as the sails filled.

'We're going to Angel Island,' he said. 'It's a beat all the way there, sailing as close to the wind as we can. Coming back we reach with the wind on the beam or we run with the wind behind us. The lines that control the sails are called sheets, so if I tell you to go forward and haul in the jib sheet you'll know what to do, yes?'

'Aye, aye, sir.'

'When we tack, I put the tiller down and I say, "Ready about!" so you'll know that the boom is going to swing to the other side and you'll get out of its way.'

'Can I jump into your lap to be safe?'

'Later, when we anchor. Ready about! Lee oh!' The boom swung around with no danger to us in the cockpit.

'Who's Leo?' I said.

'That's just an extra bit I read in a book. I learned my sailing from books. I started out with a twelve-and-a-half-foot Beetle Cat and worked my way up through a Chuckles 18 before I made the jump to *Mariposa*. I've always favoured gaff-rigged boats. They look more like boats to me, though I also like luggers.'

'Albert Pinkham Ryder painted luggers, some of them on cigar-box lids.'

'Probably not a lot of people know that. I'll google for him when I have time.'

Alternately on starboard and port tacks we beat our way to Angel Island. I mentally rehearsed various conversational gambits, rejected them all, and sat there like a sixteen-year-old on her first date, watching Jim's easy handling of the tiller and the mainsheet. His hands were large and strong but they did everything gently. The sunlight on the water was dazzling; I saw Jim through veils of brightness, and I had lapsed into a reverie when he startled me out of it.

'What's that?' he said sharply.

'What? Where?' I responded dozily.

'Three points off the port bow,' he said nautically. 'There!' he pointed.

'Walk on by,' I said when I saw what it was. 'Let it be.'

'I can't, it's a hazard to navigation.' He reached for the boat hook. 'What is it?'

'It's what Volatore Three paid a hundred and fifty thousand dollars for.'

'Wow! That's a lot of money.'

'It's a lot of tiny, tiny dancing bad luck too. I think we'll both be sorry if you pick it up.'

'Why? What could happen?' He was lifting it aboard.

'I don't know but I've got a bad feeling about it.'

'How'd it get here?'

'Jumped off the Golden Gate Bridge, I should think. Possibly an assisted suicide.'

'You've got some history with this painting, right?'

'Right, but let's save that for another time, OK?'

'OK. I'd like to take it home, though, to have a proper look at it. Take the tiller for a moment, will you – I want to tie it down so it won't blow away.'

The tiller was in my hand as he laid the painting on the cabin roof. I don't know what I did wrong then but the boom suddenly swung across to the other side and knocked Jim into the water.

'Jim!' I screamed.

I let go of the tiller and the boat came up into the wind, losing most of its forward motion as the jib fluttered indecisively and the spanker spilled its wind. The current was very strong but it carried him towards me instead of away and he was able to grab the dinghy that was trailing astern. He clambered aboard it, hauled himself up to *Mariposa* and was in my arms.

'Oh Jim!' I sobbed with relief.

The tiny, tiny dancing giants smirked in the dim red caverns of sleep on the cabin roof. Jim dropped anchor and tied down the painting. Then we took off our wet clothes and went below, where we found ourselves naked and holding on to each other.

'We are in danger of endangering the therapeutic relationship, I think,' said Jim.

'I won't tell anyone if you don't,' I murmured into his neck.

53

Hopefulness of Volatore

Is she near? I think I feel her presence! Ah! Be near, my
Angelica! Soon, perhaps, no longer apart?

54

42nd Street Buck-and-Wing

Well, it was what it was, wasn't it! I mean, sleeping with Jim was all that I wanted it to be but it didn't resolve all my problems and it didn't wrap up the story of me and Jim and tie it with a pink ribbon.

Confusion is the medium in which I live, like a fish in water. If clarity suddenly happened I don't think I could breathe. There we were with our sun-dried clothes back on. *WHAT NOW?* flashed on and off in the air like an invisible neon sign, seen perhaps by the tiny, tiny giants dancing on the cabin roof.

Why had the painting floated out to meet us? Had Volatore Three jumped off the bridge with it? He hadn't seemed a suicidal type. I was sniffing the air. No smell but maybe . . . No, nothing.

'I'd like to propose a toast,' said Jim, 'to Cyd Charisse who died yesterday. One more beauty gone from the world. Here's to you, Cyd. We'll stay danced with.'

'Here's to you, Cyd,' I echoed as my eyes filled with tears. We touched glasses and sat in silence for a moment.

'Her death hit you pretty hard?' said Jim.

'I cry very easily, and about more things all the time.'

'A burrito will dry your tears.'

I was crying because I was thinking of Ruby Keeler. My collection of DVDs of Hollywood musicals includes Fred Astaire and all the women he danced with, but further back too, the thirties and films like *42nd Street*, *Footlight Parade* and *Gold Diggers of 1935*. In *42nd Street* Ruby Keeler sings the title song and dances to it. Busby Berkeley of course designed the big numbers but this one looked as if Ruby Keeler was doing her own buck-and-wing, glowing with innocent pride in her tap dancing; her moves were such as a child might invent, full of high spirits and *joie de vivre*. This in the height of the Depression. But the general hope was that just around the corner was a rainbow in the sky. The atom bomb did not yet exist, nobody had heard of global warming and polar bears had miles and miles of ice on which to hunt seals. That's why I was crying.

Angel Island seemed, as we approached it, more crowded than we required, so we anchored well offshore and ate and drank contentedly while gently rocked on the cradle of the deep. I must have fallen asleep then because I became aware of waking up. The sky was red with sunset and Jim was watching me.

'You looked so peaceful that I didn't want to disturb you,' he said. 'You must have been having pleasant dreams.'

'I don't remember.' But there had been *something*: not a dream but an awareness that Volatore hadn't lost me, nor I him.

'I have a headline running through my mind like a tune that won't go away,' said Jim. '"SHRINK PLIED PATIENT WITH DRINK IN DATE-RAPE".'

'If you're having guilt fantasies please do it in your own time. This is still my picnic outing.'

So we picnicked and fooled around until the moon came up and we get under way again. It was a big round full moon, riding quietly in the sky with a big smile on its face.

'I arranged this for you,' said Jim.

'You think of everything,' I said, and kissed him. It was a little like faking an orgasm but you can't always be completely honest.

Jim hauled up the anchor and we headed for home. He sensed a change and became thoughtful at the tiller. The sails filled and I could see by our wake that we were moving right along but the air seemed perfectly still.

'That's because we're running now,' said Jim, 'and we're moving at the same speed as the wind.'

'Life is full of metaphors,' I said, moving at the same speed as my stillness.

55

Base Metal of Gold

So much to think about! I couldn't separate my Jim thoughts from my Volatore ones. Alone in my apartment where Volatore had first appeared at the window, I went through my regular exercise routine, did my bathroom things, downed a large Laphroaig, put de Sainte-Colombe's *Pièces de viole* in the Bose, moved Irene & Co over to give me a little room, and got into bed. Lying enveloped in those shapely shadow-sonorities centuries old. I put my mind back to that night when I saw Volatore at the window. Where was I in my life at that moment? Why was I go ready to let him in? I had to dig deep into my memory to come up with a name – it seemed to belong to a time long gone although it was actually quite recent: Michael Gold. *Dr* Michael Gold.

Everybody thought I was going to marry him. We were an obvious match: he was young, handsome, a brilliant neurosurgeon, the catch of the year, and I was considered the ideal wife for the above. It was a foregone conclusion that we were going to tie the knot pretty soon but it was not *my* foregone conclusion.

The peer-pressure and the Michael-pressure didn't leave me much wiggle room but life is not completely predictable. I was rummaging through the unindexed remnant of Dad's tottering CD stacks when I found *Der Freischütz* recorded by the Berlin Philharmonic under Joseph Keilberth with the redoubtable Rudolf Schock as Max plus a programme of the 1964 San Francisco Opera production. Also a torn-off bit of sketchbook paper on which my father had written 'the white dove'. I wondered if Dad had seen the SFO production.

I looked at the cast list from forty-four years ago. Where were Richard Cassilly (Max) and Elizabeth Mosher (Agathe) now? And Malcolm Smith (Kaspar) and David Giosso (Samiel)? Forty-four years! Not doing opera any more, I should think.

I listened to the recording, then I bought a libretto and a DVD of the 1968 Hamburg State Opera production. They did it beautifully. The singers looked good and sounded great, the sets and staging were wonderfully atmospheric and the Wolf's Glen was scary like anything, a proper place in which to invoke Samiel for the casting of magic bullets. The music – Weber is above all a colourist and the singers and the orchestra perfectly conveyed the mordant blues, the sombre browns and the darkling devilish greens of his forest and his story. Those colours were consonant with my mood at that time and I had a strong craving for them.

Here are the main elements of *Der Freischütz*:

1. Max and Agathe are in love but Cuno, Agathe's father, will only let them marry if Max wins Prince Ottokar's shooting trial the next day. If he does, he wins Agathe and succeeds Cuno as head forester. But Max has been missing all his shots lately and things look bad for him.

2. Kaspar, who has sold his soul to Samiel (the devil), sees Max drinking alone and says, 'See that eagle high in the sky? Take my gun and shoot it.'

'It's out of range,' says Max, but he fires and the eagle falls dead at his feet.

'That was a charmed bullet in his gun,' says Kaspar. 'If Max wants such bullets he must meet him in the Wolf's Glen at midnight.'

3. Despite Agathe's fears Max goes to that haunted place where even the ghost of his mother tries to warn him away. Evil apparitions surround him but he goes down to where Kaspar, invoking Samiel, is casting seven bullets. Six will fly true but the seventh is meant to kill Agathe and give Kaspar three more years before Samiel collects his soul.

4. Agathe dreams that she is a white dove and Max is aiming at her. In the morning she hurries to where Ottokar is saying, 'The white dove in that tree is your mark, Max.'

'Don't shoot!' cries Agathe. 'I am the white dove!' But Max has fired. Agathe falls, but only in a swoon. Kaspar falls from the same tree, killed by Samiel's charmed bullet.

5. Ottokar says that Max must be punished for consorting with Samiel but he asks the local holy man, a pious hermit, to decide on the sentence. Max and Agathe must stay apart for a year, says the hermit. After that they may marry. Everybody cheers and thanks God, and that's a wrap.

'The white dove', my father had written, and I knew that for him the dove was more than Agathe but I was content to let it be his private bird.

I wondered what Michael would think of *Der Freischütz* and the white dove so I invited him over for pizza and a viewing. He arrived with a big smile on his face and an airline ticket which he waved in front of me.

'What's that?' I said.

'A weekend at the Grand Mayan in Acapulco,' he chortled, 'and two business-class seats on Aviacsa's Friday-afternoon flight. One of the nurses has Mexican connections and she got me a big discount.'

Michael and I had never slept together and I'd made him keep his tongue in his mouth when he kissed me goodnight after a date. He was better at operating on other people's brains than at using his own which was mostly in his pants.

'I'm busy this weekend,' I said.

'Busy doing what?'

'Busy not going to Acapulco.'

'Come on, Angie, don't mess with me like that.'

'I'm not messing with you. There's the doorbell, the pizza's here.'

'Pizza!' he snorted.

'Don't snort,' I said. 'That's what you were invited for: pizza and *Der Freischütz*.'

'*Der Frei*-fucking-*schütz*,' he resnorted, scorning italics.

'This is Marco's pizza classica,' I said. 'Don't let it get cold. And there's Chianti Classico.'

'Pepperoni,' he said when I opened the box. 'But I like it with Hawaiian topping.'

'If I'd known you were into that kind of perversion I wouldn't have invited you. Shall I remove the pepperoni and put jam on your half?'

'That does it,' he snapped. 'I'm outta here. And I won't have any trouble getting somebody else for Acapulco.'

'I hope you'll be very happy together. Don't slam the door on your way out. *Vaya con Dios*.'

That was how we parted. And that evening a hippo-griff appeared at my window. I'll never forget my first sight of that strange beaked face and those eyes staring at me. Volatore! An imaginary creature but there he was, and in a matter of minutes I was naked on all fours under him and he covered me as the griffin had covered his mother. I screamed as his seed spurted into me, and all the while the music that had lifted him to my window was on the Bose, Olimpia lamenting her lost Bireno in the voice of Emma Kirkby.

Why and how had it happened? Had I ever since my limited reading of Ariosto nursed a subconscious passion for the hippogriff? And even if that were so, how had he broken through the membrane of his reality into mine?

Now Volatore and Jim were circling in my head like the figures in a little weather house. Who was fair weather and who was foul? I didn't know, I was burdened well over my confusion loadline and my judgement was not to be trusted.

Eventually I fell asleep and the eyes that stared at me in the darkness of my dream were those of Volatore. In utter silence he brought his face close to mine and there were tears in his eyes.

'Oh,' I said, and woke up.

56

Where from Here?

I didn't see Jim or talk to him until our next session, two days later. *Dos Arbolitos* looked at me as if she'd never seen me before.

'Don't give me that,' I said. 'We go way back.'

But I was wondering what Jim was to me now; could a lover still be your shrink? *Was* he now my lover? Or had it just been a one-boat stand?

When I went inside Jim was wearing a cardboard smile.

'Hi,' he said, syncing his lips with his voice.

'Relax,' I said. 'You look as if you're expecting my dad to turn up with a shotgun.'

'Nothing as simple as that.'

'What, then?'

'What did you dream last night?'

'Ah! I see where this is going. Let's do it like the song – you tell me your dream and I'll tell you mine.'

'I dreamed of your hippogriff, the same as you, right?'

'Why do you say that?'

'Because it felt as if it was coming from you.'

'What was he doing in your dream?'

'Looking at me with tears in his eyes. Was that your dream?'

'Yes, exactly the same. Does that surprise you?'

'Not really. When people are tuned to each other, that kind of thing can happen. It's a sort of telepathy.'

'Has it ever happened to you before?'

'No.'

'So then we're tuned to each other, right?'

'As I've said.'

'Are you comfortable with that?'

'I think there are things we need to sort out.'

'Like what?'

Jim had his notebook in his hand and was leafing through it.

'Here we are,' he said. 'The session where you said you had a reality problem and I said, "That's called life." Which seems to me now a little flippant. The fact is that I'd never had a client with your looks before and I was showing off. Trying to be cool.'

'Go on.'

'You said you were living in two realities, maybe more, and you were trying to understand them so you'd know how to deal with them. And I said that was a waste of energy, that it didn't matter how many realities there were, you just had to handle them one at a time and do whatever had to be done.'

'Perfectly sound advice, I thought. Still do.'

'Wait, now we're coming to the heart of the matter: I said that everything that happens to you – even a hallucination – is real; it's part of your reality.'

'So?'

'The thing is, Angelica, sometimes you have to let go of part of your reality. Life is, after all, a succession of losses.'

'How can you say that! Was it a loss that you and I found each other?'

'I'm talking about the loss of such things as youthful illusions; and adult delusions.'

'Get to the point, Jim.'

'Your Volatore thing, for example.'

'My Volatore *thing*? I don't believe I'm hearing this. Are you jealous, is that it?'

'I don't want your Volatore reality to interfere with the reality you and I share.'

'Are you afraid that Volatore is stronger than you are?' All sorts of thoughts were running through my mind when I said that. I remembered Vassily Baby and the ease with which he had expelled Volatore. 'Jim, are you afraid of Volatore?'

'I don't want to have to compete with him.'

'What about coexisting with him?'

'A *ménage à trois* with an imaginary animal! What a great idea! Or we could bring in the Tooth Fairy and make it a foursome, how about that?'

'All right then, you tell me what we should do.'

'I already have: lose Volatore.'

As I looked at Jim, his face didn't seem to be the one I had kissed aboard the *Mariposa*. I remembered my heartfelt relief when he climbed back on deck after being knocked overboard. Where was that relief now? And who was this stranger laying down the law for me? I knew in my heart that there was something wrong in Jim's rightness and something right in my wrongness. I may be crazy, but I feel I have a moral obligation to be true to my craziness. No matter what happened I wasn't about to give up Volatore.

I must have been silent for a while because Jim said, 'So where do we go from here?'

'Home,' I said, and left.

57

Shame and Blame

I'm ashamed of myself. Why did I behave that way with
Angelica, denying not only her beliefs but also my own?
Why this cowardice? What am I afraid of? I'm afraid of
opening myself to the same reality I've encouraged her
to accept without question. So how can I now regain my
belief in myself? I need to become as brave as Angelica.
She makes me want to be a better man than I am.

58

Ars Longa, *Cuddly Catering*

I still had my Jim problems on my mind but for the moment the Ossip Przewalski show provided a welcome distraction. Nudes on motorbikes would seem, to some art-lovers, a trashy subject, but Ossip Przewalski's paintings are definitely not trash. As I've said before, his approach is somewhere between Kokoschka and Redon, and Toby Shure, art critic of the *Chronicle*, has said of his work, 'With instinctive insight, Przewalski has reached into the Zeitgeist and come up with an image emblematic of our speed-and-sex-crazed time. These blurred and frantic female nakednesses with their elongated testosteronal steeds between their legs are the perfect eidolon of our going-to-hell-as-fast-as-possible culture.'

The place was filling up fast and the atmosphere was right. The paintings bejewelled the white walls with colour and a warm and cheerful buzz suffused the gallery. Students from the Conservatory of Music, recruited as a small string orchestra, were harmoniously stringing their way through Vivaldi's *L'estro armonico* while champagne and canapés were being dispensed by girls wearing biker jackets and little else – black bras and panties, garter belts, black stockings and boots. *CUDDLY.CATERING. COM*, said their jackets with justifiable confidence.

Olivia and I were flaunting our assets in very tight black designer jeans, high heels, pink shirts open down to here, leather biker jackets with the Eidolon logo (a spooky sibylline face) and the words *Ars longa, vita brevis est*, and visored biker caps.

Moira Lesser, Arts and Entertainment reporter for CBS5 TV, arrived with her crew to interview Ossie. Standing him in front of *Nude on Harley No. 15*, she told her viewers, I'm coming to you live from the Eidolon Gallery in downtown San Francisco where Ossip Przewalski's new show is opening.' Turning to him, she said, 'To me this painting says many things about our world, our time. Can you share with our viewers some of your thoughts when you stand before a blank canvas ready to begin?'

'Well,' said Ossie, 'at that point I have a girl and a bike in front of me. Suzie is one of my favourite models – she's a natural redhead with pale-pink areolas and a lovely bush.' Ignoring the look on Moira's face he continued smoothly, 'The bike is my new XR1200, red. Red is the quintessential motorbike colour. Think bike and you see red.'

'Yes,' said Moira, 'and if you could tell us a little about what drives you, your motivation?'

'I like naked women, I like motorbikes and I like money.'

'Thank you,' said Moira. Facing the camera then, 'I've been talking to Assip . . . Ossip Przewalski, at the opening of his new show at the Eidolon Gallery. Moira Lesser, CBS TV, San Francisco.'

She drew her finger across her throat, the crew packed up, and she and they were gone.

I might mention here that Ossie arrived at the opening of his show as Lenore Goldfarb's arm candy. She was lustrous and tinkling in full chandelier and he was in leather except for a blue denim shirt open far enough to display a tattoo of a full-frontal nude redhead on a Harley. Rumour has it that Lenore has commissioned him to paint her, presumably with a body double but her own jewellery and a naked bike.

Joe Fontana was also here by my invitation. When Lenore saw him she gave him a very hard look, doubtless recalling the fifty thousand dollars for the tiny, tinies. Joe apparently still had no recollection of her and that event.

Our usual Ossie A list had been invited. It included the local Harley Davidson CEO, high-ranking members of Hells Angels and the other clubs, the Mayor, the Chief of Police and other dignitaries. My own additions to the list were Sergeant Hennessy, Joe Fontana and Volatore Three, who brought in his wake Lola Trotter and her boyfriend, pop sin-singer Billy Viro. Dad showed up looking spruce and successful, to be hovered over by Olivia who took pains to keep both his glass and his eye filled. I had invited Jim and here he was. Explanations seemed unnecessary so we hugged and kissed without explaining.

People were mingling well, the cuddly caterers were handing out business cards and perhaps telephone numbers along with the champagne and canapés. Things were mellowing nicely and red dots were breaking out all over as Ossie's nudes sold briskly, his instinctive insights in demand as always.

Sergeant Hennessy – his name is John – arrived with his wife Kitty. He was quite handsome in a dinner jacket and I was surprised to realise that he was about the same age as Jim. Kitty was about my age and frisky. She reminded me of Ruby Keeler.

'Vivaldi might do for a reel,' she said, 'but I'm more of a buck-and-wing girl.'

'I thought you might be,' I said. 'You have a Ruby Keeler air.'

Her eyes brightened with recognition of a kindred spirit.

'You've seen *42nd Street*?'

'It's one of my favourites – I've become kind of hooked on Depression films.'

'They knew how to have fun,' said Kitty.

'Well,' said Hennessy, 'just around the corner was a rainbow in the sky. We haven't got one.'

'I'd like to learn to tap dance,' I said.

'Have you got rhythm?' said Hennessy.

'All us Jews got rhythm.'

'Call me up,' said Kitty. 'We'll have a session to give me an idea where to send you for lessons.'

Joe Fontana made his way to me looking serious. He was in good financial shape now, having bought into Marco's Pizzeria Classica, and he had time on his hands.

'I was thinking,' he said, 'of taking up painting.'

'Your former patron is here,' I said. 'Lenore Goldfarb. Name ring any bells?'

'None that I can hear.'

'But you're thinking of taking up painting. Having dreams?' I said.

'More like something I almost remember.'

'Don't give up your day job,' said Hennessy.

'I haven't got one,' said Joe. 'All I do is collect money from my share of the business.'

'Why'd Renzetti sell off a third interest in the place?' said Hennessy.

'He wants to spend more time coaching a kids' rugby team that he organised.'

'I don't suppose painting as a hobby can do any harm to you or the general public,' I said to Joe. 'Just be careful.'

'If you start smelling mostly like a horse, give me a ring,' said Hennessy.

'I will,' said Joe. He thanked us and drifted away.

'You guys probably have things to talk about,' said Kitty. 'I'm going to look at the paintings and maybe find some champagne.'

The crowd was thinning out.

'I used to have an impulse to climb into your lap and tell you my troubles,' I said to Hennessy.

'Looks as if you might have found a better lap,' he replied, grinning at Jim.

'Do my best,' said Jim.

We left together and he did.

59

Jim on the Brim

The painting I fished out of the water. I haven't really looked at it since I brought it home. Angelica said it was a lot of tiny, tiny dancing bad luck and we'd both be sorry if I picked it up. Did it try to drown me? The boom knocked me overboard when she let go of the tiller. Had I told her what happens when you do that? Now I can't be sure. Anyhow, this seems like a good time to see what's what with this thing.

60

Paradise Lost

I wanted to know how (and if) things were with Volatore Three, the hairstylist and inventor of TurboScalp. I still had his card so I invited him round to the gallery for drinks. In view of the fact that the hundred-and-fifty-thousand-dollar painting had turned up in San Francisco Bay I thought he might be in a delicate state and would be glad to avoid the hurly-burly of a more public watering place. We were in the process of taking down Ossie Przewalski's show but I doubted that the hairstylist would be disturbed by a roomful of nudes on Harley Davidsons.

Remembering Volatore Three's grandiosity, I was surprised and saddened by his present appearance. He had always been a small man but this afternoon he seemed so diminished that I could have sworn he'd lost a couple of inches. His wig looked dispirited; his Armani hung loosely on him; his Rolex, I guessed, had no good times to offer and apparently his Mont Blanc and fat cheque-book could buy him no joy.

We sat him down at a little table with a bottle of Sancerre and a plate of sandwiches. Olivia and I raised our glasses to him.

'Here's luck,' I said.

He responded with a weary nod.

'How are you?' I said.

He shrugged and made the universal so-so gesture with the flat of his hand.

'So-so,' he said. '*Cosi-cosi.*'

'Did you,' I tried to say very gently, 'drop the painting off the Golden Gate Bridge?'

He nodded.

'It was either it or me. I was poised to make the jump myself but a large policeman convinced me that the wind conditions were not right and I might fatally injure one of the yachtsmen below us. He gave me his card and invited me to have coffee with him to talk the matter over. I began to think about how foolish I should look falling through the air with my toupee flying off, so I decided to go on living a while longer.'

'You mean that isn't your own hair?' said Olivia.

He shook his head and smiled modestly.

'Amazing,' I said. 'Tell me, was the policeman's name Hennessy?'

'Yes. How did you know?'

'I know him, and it's the kind of thing he would do.'

'Can you tell us what happened?' said Olivia. 'The last time we saw you, you liked that painting well enough to pay a hundred and fifty thousand dollars for it.'

'The tiny, tiny dancing giants in the dim red caverns of sleep,' he murmured, and held out his empty glass which I quickly refilled. 'There was with me when I bought the painting a feeling' – he spread his arms as if to embrace the world – 'of an immensity of comprehension, of containing in myself the whole dream of reality which is the world.'

Olivia and I had nothing to say; we were both eating the little sandwiches to fill the emptiness we suddenly felt.

Silence. I offered the plate of sandwiches to Volatore Three. He shook his head and took more wine.

'Please go on,' I said. 'What happened then?'

He put down his glass and covered his face with his hands.

'It left me, the immensity of comprehension suddenly was gone from me like a dream I couldn't remember. The painting closed up and went flat.' He took his hands away and I got another bottle of wine. 'You can't imagine my loss,' he said, 'unless you've contained that immensity and experienced the same loss.'

More silence.

'TurboScalp?' I said hesitantly. 'Does that help at all?'

'It works only if you think it will. And I don't think it will.'

'How's your translation of *Orlando Furioso* going?' said Olivia.

'I seem to have lost my flair for rhyming. Thank you for your hospitality. I shall leave you now.'

'Come see us again,' I said.

Volatore Three bowed, kissed our hands, and headed for the door. We watched him get smaller and smaller and then he was gone.

61

Mental Jimnastics

The painting of the tiny, tiny dancing giants in the dim red caverns of sleep: the words alone make you want to lean against a wall. This painting affects different people in different ways: Joe Fontana, who had never painted before, created it in an altered state, calling himself Volatore and smelling like Volatore. He later reverted to his normal state with no recollection of doing the painting nor of selling it to Lenore Goldfarb. When Hennessy and Angelica took him to the gallery and made him look at it he fainted.

Volatore Three dreamed about the tiny tinies and followed their metaphysical scent to the gallery. Looking at the painting seemed to have no physical effect on him while he was in the altered and smelly state. When he reverted to his normal state he threw the painting off the Golden Gate Bridge.

Lenore Goldfarb paid Joe Fontana fifty thousand dollars for the painting but then developed an aversion to it without going strange or smelly and wanted it out of the house.

Alexander Zhabotinsky had never seen the painting but spoke of 'winey, winey trancing clients in the dim red taverns of sheep' and took on the famous smell very briefly. As his normal state, however, is already altered from what most people would call normal it is not possible to assess the effect, if any, on him.

Hennessy, Angelica and Olivia all felt woozy looking at it but no more than that. I had to sit down quickly when I first looked directly at it.

So, reviewing these data, what do I think? I think the painting puts into an altered state only those who come more than halfway to meet it, those who want something from it, perhaps access to that dream of reality made real in it. Joe Fontana and Volatore Three went more than halfway to meet it and what happened? It took them in and then it spat them out. So the painting has opinions, it decides whom to accept and whom to reject. What is it looking for, what does it want?

What is the genius of the painting, its familiar spirit or whatever that made Joe Fontana, not an artist, visualise the tiny, tiny dancing giants in the dim red caverns of sleep? Whatever it is, it's something that wants to, needs to? make itself known to some but not to others.

Lenore Goldfarb, Hennessy, Angelica and Olivia were not invited in; they didn't need what it had to offer. They were already based on the reality necessary to them.

Well, we'll see what happens when Dr Jim steps up to the plate.

62

Between Jim and It

The painting was in the bedroom, with its face to the wall it was leaning against. I hadn't looked at it since bringing it home. When I fished it out of the water and laid it on the cabin roof it was just a big canvas on stretchers, nothing more than that. But now it seemed to be waiting for me. Well, I had done that to myself, hadn't I, by leaning it against the wall and making it wait. But now the evening seemed favourable; I'd seen my last client for the day, a woman who constantly used the word 'relationship' and the phrase 'more importantly'. She also liked using singular verbs with plural subjects and she thought the nominative case classier than the objective case. 'Between you and I,' she said in a burst of emotion, 'there's many, many guys out there who will simply not commit to a relationship. More importantly, I have issues of my own with commitment in a relationship. You know what I'm saying?'

'I think so,' I said. 'More importantly, I've been taking notes so I can go over your issues again.'

She seemed well satisfied with the therapeutic relationship but I was very tired after the session. I poured myself a large Jack Daniel's, sighed and returned to the matter of the painting.

'OK,' I said, 'I'm ready.'

I brought it into my office and stood it on the sofa facing me. I had to look away then and sit down because I lost my balance and almost fell over.

'Obviously I'm not going at this correctly,' I said. As I said that I could feel what the correct approach was but I wasn't ready to commit to the relationship the tiny, tiny dancing giants seemed to want. Not looking directly at the painting I said to it, 'I'm going to have to think about this, OK? I'll get back to you.' I took it into the bedroom again and leant it against the wall as before.

63

Blondin Not

In 1859 Blondin crossed Niagara Falls on a tightrope. It makes my feet tingle just to think of it and I can hear the roar of the Falls. He had a balance pole, I can feel the weight of it in my hands, with Jim on one end of it and Volatore on the other as I cross my Niagara, not daring to look down and not altogether confident of reaching the other side. Thinking, meanwhile, that I didn't ask for this. Did I?

64

Patience of Volatore

Time is on my side and I can wait. Have I not already waited centuries? Closer and closer, Angelica! Faster and faster runs the sand through the glass!

Careful, Volatore! '*Chi va piano, va sano.*' Luck is a frail craft, and the Sea of Chance has not only storms to sink the unwary but also windless days to weary the spirit.

65

Jimportantly, A Commitment

'OK,' I said to the Jack Daniel's bottle, 'you know and I know that the only way to get on the other side of this thing is to go through it, right?'

Getting no argument from Jack I fortified myself as required, strode into the bedroom and laid hands on the painting. So far, so good.

I took it into the office, set it on the sofa as before, and sat down without looking at it. Then, after a brief consultation with Dr Daniel I turned the full power of my trepidation on the painting. While I held on to the desk to keep from falling out of my chair I asked myself: Why was I trepidating? I think we know instinctively, all of us, when we are going into something from which there is no way back. So the question arises: Do I want to get to that place from which there is no return? From that question arises a second question: Do I have a choice? And a third question: Why do I have to bother with this painting at all? Angelica has warned me that it's a lot of bad luck. But my instincts are telling me that it is also the way to make Angelica mine.

Where I am now is like being in a flooded cave and what looks like the only way out is to swim underwater through a narrow tunnel towards a faint glimmer which may or may not be daylight. And you wonder if you can hold your breath long enough.

So how much do I want Angelica and am I a man or a coward? OK, Jack. One for the road and in I go.

66

Impatience of Volatore

Something is happening! Something is approaching!
Closer, closer, don't hang back! Closer, closer, closer!
Here I am, here is Volatore waiting!

67

Jim-Jammed?

OK, guys, this is it, you and me *mano a mano*. You're on the sofa, I'm at my desk. Here's looking at you dim red tinies. Do whatever you're going to do.

Queasiness, uneasiness. Dimness, redness, cavernous sleep. Dream-dancing the dream of . . . what? Dancing, dancing. Tinily gigantic, I also redly dim Jim. What Jim? This Jim. What this? Suddenly! an immensity of comprehension, of containing in myself the whole dream of reality which is the world.

Oho! So farther, deeper? No, I don't, yes, I do but wait. What? What entering? Entering me but I'm not, I haven't, I don't but aah, the tiny, tiny dancing jim-jams! But this other. Not tiny, very big. Well, no use locking the barn door after the horse is inside.

68

Cautious Optimism of Volatore

Dare I hope? The way has been so long and hard! You old gods, forgotten by the world, hear my humble prayer!

69

Jam Today

This was my regular session day so I went. It was two days after the night of Ossie Przewalski's opening and everything was fine between Jim and me but I was wondering and worrying about how matters stood with Volatore and me. The last thing I wanted was to have to choose between my two lovers and I was afraid of losing both. The ferry ride to Sausalito this morning felt different from ferry rides on other mornings. The day was hard and bright, the sunlight unyielding, the sun points on the water were like dancing shards of glass. The gulls were laughing at me, 'Haha, haha-ha! Haha!'

'Stupid garbage-eaters!' I said. 'Who the hell are you to haha at me?'

'Today, today!' screamed the gulls.

'Today what?'

'Um maybe yes, maybe no,' thrummed the engines. 'Um maybe maybe maybe.'

'Nobody asked you,' I told them.

When the ferry docked there was nothing to do but get off so I did that. All the way to *Dos Arbolitos* I was talking to myself. Sometimes people stared at me and I realised that I was speaking out loud. Why so freaked out? I asked myself. This is only the rest of my life we're talking about here.

Then all of a sudden *Dos Arbolitos* was in front of me. I went in and Jim came to meet me. With, yes, the smell!

'Volatore!' I said. 'Is that you?'

'Here is Volatore,' he said.

He took me in his arms and everything became all right.

Since then I've had no complaints. Sometimes Jim is plain Jim and sometimes he's Volatore Jim. Well, really, every good man is a bit of an animal and every animal has something human about it. Reader, I married them.

70

Dancing in the Dark

What became of that infamous painting that passed from hand to hand and went swimming in San Francisco Bay? Volatore Two (Joe Fontana) painted it. He had never painted a picture before, and later could not recall doing it. Lenore Goldfarb paid a hundred and fifty thousand dollars for it, then couldn't stand the sight of it. Volatore Three bought it next. At first it filled him with an immensity of comprehension, a feeling that he contained in himself the whole dream of reality which is the world. Then it almost made him jump off the Golden Gate Bridge. Angelica Greenberg and Olivia Partridge felt woozy viewing it, as did Sergeant Hennessy. When Joe Fontana was taken to the Eidolon Gallery and forced to look at what he had painted he fainted. Alyosha Zhabotinsky picked up random snatches of the idea of it and suffered no ill effects. Jim Long experienced the immensity of comprehension but was occupied by Volatore One before any come down from the immensity.

What was to be done with *Tiny, Tiny Dancing Giants in the Dim Red Caverns of Sleep*? To sell it to anyone would be irresponsible; to give it to a charity would be uncharitable. After long thought Dr Jimatore wrapped it in two thicknesses of brown paper and locked it in a *Dos Arbolitos* cupboard, the resting-place of a broken beach-umbrella, a retired croquet set and a Ouija board.

71

Passage to El Paso

The Chicano Collection is the current exhibition at
the El Paso Museum of Art. Christian Gerstheimer, the
curator, has been showing visitors through the galleries
daily. This morning, in his office checking his messages,
he finds himself thinking of where he is in the world.
El Paso, the Pass, is on the Rio Bravo del Norte, the
Rio Grande, facing Juarez across the river which flows
through Texas to the sea. Beyond Juarez stand the mountains. Mountains beyond the river that flows to the sea.
El Paso, the sound of horses is in the name, the whinny-
ing and the hoofbeats, the creak of leather and the cries
of riders riding to the sea. El Paso. Why these thoughts?
No idea.

He passes through the galleries to where *Ruggiero Saves*
Angelica, tempera on wood by Girolamo da Carpi, hangs,
hearing his footsteps on the hardwood floor and thinking, as he has never thought before, how many millions,

billions, countless trillions of footsteps there have been since the world began. Under the nocturnal daylight of the halogen lamps the silent faces in the paintings have no answers.

Michelle Villa, the Registrar of the El Paso Museum of Art, driving from her house in Kern Place three miles away, takes Mesa Street past the University of Texas at El Paso, and continues through the architectural reminiscings of Sunset Heights. The pale browns of the urban palette are picked up in painterly fashion by the distant-background brown ridges of the Franklin Mountains beyond Jaurez across the Rio Bravo. The air is dry, the day is windy and the wind shakes the stacked sombreros and flutters the rebozos of the street vendors. Michelle thinks of how the dry wind and the distant brown mountains will go with her little daughter Astrid wherever she goes as a grown-up Astrid with perhaps a childhood rebozo carefully folded in a drawer.

As often happens, the tide of her travelling thoughts has brought her to the beach of the working day and here she is in the museum.

Christian Gerstheimer pauses before the da Carpi. Something has caught his eye. What? He doesn't know. With his right arm bent at the elbow, the forearm across his stomach, his left elbow resting on it and his left hand cradling his chin, he contemplates the painting in the classic stance of a man contemplating a painting. Minutes pass and so does Michelle Villa.

'Have a look at this,' he says.

She takes up a stance identical to his. Minutes pass.

'Well?' says Gerstheimer. 'See anything different about the picture?'

'Yes.'

'What?'

'You'll think I've gone crazy.'

'No, I won't, I promise. Tell me what you see.'

'OK,' says Michelle. 'Maybe I *have* gone crazy.'

'Please, Michelle!'

'All right then, it looks to me as if Angelica is smiling.'

'Really! But she's almost in profile, her features not all that distinct. How can you make out a smile?'

'I'm telling you how it looks to me, Christian.'

Gerstheimer says, 'To me *something* seems different but I couldn't say what it is. Maybe the lighting is funny today.'

Nick Muñoz, Museum Preparator is passing. Beckoned by Gerstheimer, he too takes up the stance, and now the three of them are contemplating *Ruggiero Saves Angelica*.

'Well,' says Gerstheimer, 'what do you think?'

'It looks different,' says Muñoz.

'How?' says Gerstheimer.

Muñoz begins to hum 'Volare'.

'What's that tune you're humming?' says Gerstheimer.

'Was I humming?' says Muñoz. 'I wasn't aware of it. Maybe the colours seem deeper and more vibrant.'

'I wonder if we should send it to New York to be examined by the Kress Foundation conservation labs at NYU,' says Gerstheimer.

'No need,' says Muñoz with his nose very close to the painting. 'I can *smell* if a painting's been tampered with and I haven't been wrong yet. Nothing's been done to this one but to me the colour *does* seem different. Maybe it's my eyes.'

'We're all tired from this Chicano show,' says Gerstheimer. 'Maybe tomorrow it'll look the same as always.'

The two men depart while Michelle Villa continues to contemplate the painting.

'That still looks like a smile to me,' she says.

ACKNOWLEDGEMENTS

'Why San Francisco?' you may ask. Well, when it turned out that Marco Renzetti was going there, Volatore had perforce to go along. I have never been to that city, so I had to rely on the goodwill of friends, the kindness of strangers, and Google. Along the way, people in two places allowed me, with gallantry well beyond the call of duty, to put fictionnal words in their real mouths. At the El Paso Museum of Art, curator Christian Gerstheimer, registrar Michelle Villa and preparator Nick Muñoz graced my last chapter with their presence. Michelle also gave me visual notes on El Paso, as did my son, Brom Hoban. At KDFC in San Francisco Bill Leuth asked Hoyt Smith on my behalf to allow similar fictionalisation, which he graciously agreed to.

I turned up suddenly in various San Francisco telephones and was unfailingly received with courtesy and co-operation. Becky Swanson, Wine Director at Delfina, told me not only about food and drink but also what music was being played in the restaurant. Annie Glyer at Noe Valley Pet Co. told me what Angelica would need for Irene Cat. Bill Hughes at Schoonmaker Marina told me about wind and tide in San Francisco Bay. Robert Tachetto at the Giant Camera gave me details of that obscura establishment.

Eli Bishop in San Francisco put in a lot of time and mileage to provide me with on-the-spot observation wherever needed. Endlessly patient and reliably accurate, he was my private eyes.

My wife Gundula helped me with fashion notes and all kinds of information I couldn't get for myself.

Liz Calder read my first draft and her advice helped me to get the manuscript into better shape.

Bill Swainson patiently put up with my various inserts and revisions after the manuscript was delivered as final.

Phoebe Hoban gave me useful suggestions for amplifying the text in several places.

Dominic Power read successive drafts and cheered me on at our monthly lunches at Il Fornello.

I work without an outline or overall plan, flying by the seat of my pants. Sometimes the pants wear thin and my inertial guidance system loses its way. Jake Wilson, reading my pages as I worked, kept me more than once from walking over a cliff.

Barbara Reynolds's wonderful rendering of *Orlando Furioso* into English in the Penguin Classics editon was, in its humour and *joie de vivre*, a constant inspiration.

RH
12 May 2010

A NOTE ON THE AUTHOR

Russell Hoban is the author of many extraordinary novels including *Turtle Diary, Riddley Walker, Amaryllis Night and Day, The Bat Tattoo, Her Name Was Lola, Come Dance with Me* and, most recently, *My Tango with Barbara Strozzi*. He has also written some classic books for children including *The Mouse and His Child* and the *Frances* books. He lives in London.

A NOTE ON THE TYPE

The text of this book is set in Bembo. This type was first used in 1495 by the Venetian printer Aldus Manutius for Cardinal Bembo's *De Aetna*, and was cut for Manutius by Francesco Griffo. It was one of the types used by Claude Garamond (1480–1561) as a model for his Romain de l'Université, and so it was the forerunner of what became standard European type for the following two centuries. Its modern form follows the original types and was designed for Monotype in 1929.